Private Lessons

A Temptation Press Anthology

Private Lessons

An Erotic Collection of Short Stories

A Temptation Press Anthology

TEMPTATION
PRESS

Acknowledgements

Temptation Press would like to thank all those that contributed to this anthology. We chose to showcase six new voices that best represented our vision for this work.

We would also like to thank our Temptation Press team for all their dedication and hard work to thcsc projects.

Contents

Fighting Claustrophobia

Robert Nelis

The president of Belfort Chemicals, Jerry Belfort, called me into his office and said, "You get to visit Clover, Iowa two weeks from now."

I raised my eyebrows, "Jerry, Clover in Iowa? The whole weekend?"

"Look Scott I'm stuck. My daughter is graduating from college that weekend so you'll have to go to Mid-Iowa Fertilizer's summer kick-off convention and deliver the seminar on our ABJ 40 supplement."

"The President, Ronnie Porski, always puts on a big social wingding Saturday night. You need to show our flag, attend, and spread Belfort's virtues," he smiled.

I snickered. "What the hell does one do in Clover, Iowa after the party that no doubt ends at 9:30 p.m.?"

"You're divorced, but I doubt any social action exists in Clover, so take a book. If that does not work, Belfort will cover your bar bill." Laughing he slapped his hand on his desk.

I gazed at the ceiling and shook while deliberately making an unhappy facial expression. Little did I know how wrong Jerry was to be proven.

I saw many people during the convention's seminars secessions, but the number of people attending the social kick-off surprised me; I guessed at least three-hundred. The Clover Motel's management placed one open bar in each of the hall's corners and centered three islands in the middle; two presented *hors-d'oeuvres,* and a chef carved prime rib on the middle one. Ronnie invited everyone involved in production or distribution of his products, local dignitaries, and large-scale customers.

My job required approaching groups of people and performing the introduction along with a product push routine. Some of the groups stopped their conversations and joined the introductions; others didn't want to be bothered by me and finished their conversations before even recognizing my approach. The last group I visited was of the latter type.

The four ladies intently concentrated on a hot bit of gossip. I waited, while the women finished discussing a lady—with a very prominent husband

and family—who had just been discovered standing naked in the Fire Chief's office. One said, "You know some people always respond to the fire bell!" They all laughed.

Maybe a person's ability to conduct polite social conversations with strangers wears thin after several hours of promoting a product. I found being completely ignored a little irritating. I could not help saying, "Well ladies, naughty women should be spanked, correct?"

All four women looked stunned. A very awkward silence followed as they stared at the deliverer of a totally unwanted intrusion. I immediately kicked into my introduction routine, which received a very cool reception.

As the group broke up, one of the ladies took a moment to give me a very tight-eyed look. She then turned away.

At about nine p.m. people began to depart. I stood by the door gathering up the Belfort brochures from the information table when the hard-eyed woman from the last encounter walked up.

"I'm Nicole," her face defiantly softened from our first encounter. She looked to be in her early forties, had blond-tipped hair, blue eyes, and an attractive body shape appropriate for her age.

"Scott," as we shook hands. "I apologized if my off-handed comment was offensive."

With a sincere face, she asked, "Do you really think bad women should be spanked?"

With surprise, "Ah … yes, I do."

"Oh." She looked at the floor. "What room are you in?"

"247 and I have some cold champagne." I had planned to drink the whole thing myself.

She waved her hand and walked away.

I sat in my room wondering. A local station broadcasted a west coast baseball game, so I decided to wait out a couple of innings before opening the bottle and drinking myself into a mild stupor. A little after nine-thirty a gentle knock occurred.

A red-haired woman wearing a long dark brown trench coat and tinted glasses stood at my door. I never employed hookers, so I guessed she must be a joke sent by my boss. Due to surprise, I did not block the door as she said, "Hi, Scott," and walked in.

She reached the center of the room, turned, took off the glasses, and shot a questioning look at me. "You don't recognize me." She laughed removing her coat and then slowly pulled off the red-haired wig. It was Nicole.

She smiled, "Small towns have many eyes, so a disguise is required." After a small snicker, "I remember talk of cold champagne?"

She wore business informal tan pants, a light green silk-looking blouse and a reddish scarf with tan and green highlights. I sat on the bed, and I pointed to the room's one desk chair. "Please sit down and answer my curiosity."

She sat but on the edge of the chair and gripped it's two armrests. "Well, it is related to two types of claustrophobia." She then explained how her ex-husband captained the high school football team and she acted as the head cheerleader. They had dated, went to prom, and then attended the same university. He joined the premier fraternity and she the equal sorority. They drifted apart during the middle two years but reconnected when seniors. They married in a huge ceremony the June after graduation. The wedding held Clover-wide impact because it affirmed its belief in itself.

Her dad owned the biggest employer in town— a plastic parts manufacturing company—and she held one of its Board of Directors positions. The ex-husband took a management position and became the heir apparent. "We had our children quickly to get the family thing out of the way." She raised her hands and mimicked quotations marks around the words "family thing." She shifted in the chair and then returned to grasping the armrests.

"We had the three kids in six years and seemed to be living the ideal life. Very nice big house, assured job, many friends, macho golf buddies, and clearly definable place in the community. This cruised along for about five years … when he changed."

She tilted her head to the side and combed some hair behind an ear. She continued, "In short, he became claustrophobic about his life here. Through business acquaintances and men his own age he met at conventions, he became enamored with a much broader lifestyle than Clover offered. I sensed his increasing distance, but guessed it was typical of established marriages."

She made a slight shrug of her shoulders. "One day I came home and found an envelope on the table. In the enclosed letter, he said he was leaving. He had purchased a car in secret and withdrawn $35,000 from our stock account. It also contained a document granting me a divorce, the asset division of which gave him the car and cash. That meant I retained the house, two cars, and my future stock inheritance. He went on to explain the predictability of his life's next thirty years and said it could no longer be tolerated. With no disrespect to me, but for his own mental health, he needed to cut all ties and move on. He never made contact again."

I now swung my feet to the floor and put my elbows on my knees. I raised my eyebrows, "Well that is not contagious, what's the second kind of claustrophobia?"

She stood up and walked over to the now curtain covered windows. Turning, "I have goodie-two-shoes claustrophobia."

I dropped my hands and shook my head. "What? That's a new one on me."

She raised her arms and hands to point at me. "I am the community's wronged princess. People feel sorry for me. But, and this is the big but, they expect me to carry nobly on. Work at Dad's corporation, be an excellent mother, undertake some community service, and be absolutely celibate. On top of that, I'm expected to maintain a positive attitude and basically be happy all of the time!"

She walked over and flopped into the chair. "It's hard. I usually get involved in some community or social activity once a weekend. The other night I'm alone. Compensation comes from a bottle of wine. But the princess cannot be a drinker. Every couple of months, I drive over to Iowa City and purchase three cases of wine. I have to close the garage door, so no one sees me unload the boxes. In addition, I've adopted several techniques to throw out the empty bottles in other people's garbage. Ridiculous as that sounds, its necessary for the princess image."

"I cannot date because no local unattached prince level men exist. Shit." She slapped her leg with a hand. "Once, my parents babysat the kids when I told everyone I was taking a week's vacation with an old college friend. Actually, I went by myself to one of those adult play vacation resorts. You can drink and screw for five days. I can't describe the hollow feeling that gives you. That leaves sex toys and adult movies purchased online. Damn."

She stood, again moved to the window and gazed at the farm fields through the crack in the curtains. After a moment, she faced me. "That is the life of a small town wronged princess. It's claustrophobic."

Returning to the chair, "I've been fucking good, exemplary good for five years … and have grown fucking tired of it." Putting her elbows on her knees, she gave me direct eye contact. "I want to be bad. You are a prince level stranger with no local attachments. Your comment about spanking a bad woman—"

"Made you come over tonight."

She nodded her head.

I stood up and smiled. "The glasses are actually hard plastic, but the champagne is cold." I turned my back to open the bottle and poured two glasses. I faced her again but stopped before handing her one.

"A bad woman should not drink champagne while wearing a silk blouse buttoned to her neck with a scarf on top of that. Take the blouse and scarf off then we shall taste the good stuff."

At first, she stood stiffly with a mildly surprised facial expression; it slowly melted into a very tight smile. After slinging the scarf on the chair, she unbuttoned her blouse and tossed it next to the scarf. Looking right at me with expectancy in her eyes, she unclipped her bra and let it drop to the floor.

Her breasts were full and dipped a little; they had provided milk for three children. I walked over to her with the glass but lightly rubbed each nipple with the back of my hand. She blushed as they became erect. "They droop some," she whispered.

I handed her the glass, then lightly cupped her left one. "You look like quite a woman to me. These will be fun to play with." I then lifted my glass in a toasting gesture, and she touched mine with hers.

My experience has shown me that champagne acts like a relaxing aphrodisiac. I directed her to sit on the bed, and we talked about Clover while finishing the first glass. I enjoyed watching her trying to remain politely social while still being topless. Her body language clearly showed agitation.

She put the empty glass on the bed. "You seem to like looking at my breasts."

"That's only because I have not seen the rest of you."

She let out a quiet sigh, stood up, faced me, and slowly took off her pants. She wore thong underpants and looked a question at me. I pointed at them, then at the floor. She slid them off.

I waved her over to me and placed my hands on her slightly plump hips. When my hands touched her, I could hear a slight intake of breath. I turned her so she sat on the bed with her legs hanging over the edge then pushed her back onto the bed.

Bending I gave her the first of several increasingly passionate kisses. Leaning back on my elbows, I said, "I am a breast man, and yours invite me." As I massaged and kissed them, Nicole's breathing became faster.

I slipped my fingers into her crotch, and its wetness indicated readiness. As I rubbed, her arms squeezed me closer so my lips came against hers. It was now my turn to take a breath. "Well young lady, you are going to be punished … not for something you did … but for something you are about to do. I sat up and reached out my hand, and Nicole placed her slightly shaking one in mine.

I gently pulled until she stood next to my knees. "Bend over." She did not hesitate. Her hips had to be adjusted so her butt hung right over the edge of my knees before I could start.

The pattern was simple. Four light slaps then a rub. Four more slightly harder, then another rub. I continued the rhythm and escalated the hardness. After a few minutes, her cheeks became a healthy pink color. Her hands were grasping the bed cover, and the moans became louder as we progressed.

"Your ass cheeks are beautiful as they bounce after each stroke. I'm getting hard. Four more and we are done." She let out a quiet "ouch," after each of these.

I took a few deep breaths, "Okay Nicole, stand up and kneel between my legs. You've had all the fun, now it's my turn." I unbuttoned my shirt, and she loosened my belt, opened my pants, and took out my erect penis. Without any hesitation, she put me in her mouth. The lady certainly possessed some skill, and not wanting to explode in her mouth, I pushed her off me.

"Now lie face down on the bed." I knelt down and licked some of the reddened parts of her buttocks placing several kisses on each one. Nicole was panting as I flipped her onto her back.

She hissed, "Can't you put that thing in me." With a grin, I complied and entered a very wet vagina. After about twelve strokes her vagina and leg muscles contracted to a point I could no longer move. When her body began to relax, I made several more strokes then came. My normal orgasms are great, but every once in a while, I have one that feels like all of my sexual pipes are empty. I had one of those.

I rolled onto the bed. Neither of us moved for a few minutes. When her breathing reached an almost normal level, she said, "I need some champagne."

We both crawled up toward the headboard. I poured a glass for each of us. I put my arm around her shoulders, and we again clinked glasses. For a few moments, the only thing Nicole said was, "Wow."

We snuggled for a good fifteen minutes and began to discuss the fun we just experienced. "I think you earned a 'bad girl' certification."

Her face projected humor. "Well, Scott, we certainly cracked my claustrophobia."

When I offered her a third glass, she looked at the clock and firmly stated she had to get home before the babysitter's curfew.

I sat naked on the foot of the bed holding the bottle and my glass. I watched her dress then put on the red wig, long brown coat, and sunglasses.

She tilted up the glasses and walked over to me. She kissed me. "You earned the last two glasses in the bottle." Her eyes sparkled when she twisted to look at me from the door.

"Nicole," I said with a smile, "You were naughty tonight."

"Good night, Scott. I am really glad I visited." I raised my glass in salute.

Ronnie Porski also sponsored a substantial Sunday brunch. It started right after the Anglican Church's ten a.m. mass. Recognizing my continued responsibility of promoting Belfort, it would require my attendance. I figured that being raised as a Lutheran would not preclude me from attending this mass.

After the service, I was walking around and socializing, then I saw Ronnie standing next to a woman. Several children scurried about them. She wore a white, wide-brimmed straw spring hat with a light green dress. When I approached, they both turned around. It was Nicole, and her eyes widened.

"Ah … Scott, let introduce you to one of my best Board members, Nicole Redman. Scott sells us ABJ 40 that I've told you about, it enhances the fertilizer."

I made my best correct social smile, extended my hand, and said, "I'm pleased to formally meet you. I believe we had a very brief discussion last night."

With a slightly stiff smile, she responded, "Yes, I do remember, but it is nice to actually meet you. Ronnie told the Board about the beneficial impacts of your product."

Ronnie pointed at the Church, "I hope our Priest did not bore you."

"Oh no, but we Lutherans normally have cushions on the pews. Yours are hard."

Nicole added, "You know for some reason I also found the seats to be very hard today."

Laughing Ronnie commented, "You and I have been sitting on those pews all of our lives. Don't let some soft outsider start talking of luxury praying."

A child ran up and bumped into her. "Robert is one of my three hellions. The sugar cookies encourage running around." She made a sweet smile.

"I have to say good-bye to the Smithsons," said Ronnie, "so please excuse me."

With her correct social smile, Nicole asked, "Have you found Clover to be a pleasant place?"

"I have truly enjoyed my stay here."

Her eyes glowed as we both controlled tight smiles. "I'm glad. I believe you will be leaving Clover soon, it was nice to meet you, Scott."

I nodded then offered, "If your duties ever require visiting Chicago, I'm sure Belfort would be glad to buy your dinner."

She smiled, turned, corralled Robert, and walked away.

Growing Lessons

JL Higgs

"You don't remember where the car is, do you?"

"Of course, I do."

Marcus looked at Rebecca across the rooftop of a yellow T-Bird. Then his eyes resumed searching.

"Okay. I don't," he confessed.

She laughed, her bright eyes crinkling in their corners. He joined in the laughter.

Without warning, rain began falling. They dashed through the parking lot, taking shelter beneath the mall's portico. Raindrops ran down his light brown face as the end of summer shower turned into a downpour. She folded her arms across her soaked, clinging white shirt, and he imagined wrapping his around her, their bodies touching.

Reaching behind her head, she grabbed hold of her drenched, thick wavy brown hair and lifted it from her neck. Looking at her bare suntanned skin, he wanted to touch his lips to her neck and flick aside the curled wisps of hair lying there with his tongue.

"I think it's ending," she said. "We should find the car."

"I'll write," he said. "And you'll write back. Won't you?"

Him

I sensed a change. So, I opened my eyes, and there she was, leaning against the door.

"I heard music and …"

"That's okay," I said.

She introduced herself. But I knew who she was. I'd seen her standing outside her classroom. She asked if the song was something I'd written. Then she asked me to play something else. Before I could reply, she scooted a chair over and sat her worn leather briefcase and shoulder bag on the floor.

I looked into her eyes. They were hazel, bright, and smiling. So, I placed my fingers on the piano keys and began playing. When the song ended, she touched my hand and said it was beautiful. We talked, and an unfamiliar feeling started growing inside me. Time passed unnoticed until she said she had to go. After she left, I sat there knowing something within me had changed. I didn't know what. But I wanted whatever this new thing was to last.

After that day, whenever I saw her, she smiled and waved. I thought about her constantly and hoped to spend more time talking with her, but that never worked out.

When school ended, I hadn't expected to ever see her again. Then, one day, she was in the Garden Center looking to buy tomato plant fertilizer. I showed her what we stocked and suggested she apply it that weekend since the forecast was clear. She finished paying and was leaving when I said, "Would you like to go to the beach?" She stared at me with an odd expression, so I explained my plans with friends had fallen through. Just when I thought it had been stupid to ask her to the beach, she said yes.

Her

School was over for the day. I was leaving when the sound of a piano and a baritone voice made me stop. I went to the door of the music room, opened it, and slipped inside. At the piano was a boy I didn't know. He looked nothing like Steven, but together, the piano and his voice had that same familiar, sensual and intense emotion.

When the song ended, he sat for a moment, turned his head, and looked right at me.

"I heard the music," I said by way of explanation. "Did you write that?"

He nodded.

"Would you play something else?" I asked. "By the way, I'm Rebecca Stein."

"Marcus," he said, following a lengthy pause.

He began playing, and the past and present merged into one.

After my father died, my mother had resumed teaching piano. Steven had been one of her students. Having listened to years of miss played notes and offbeat tempos, I'd learned to block out the sounds coming from her studio. But that mid-July afternoon, a heartfelt, pure, and honest song captured my attention.

When Steven was leaving after his lesson, I asked him what he'd been playing.

"Something I'm working on," he said softly.

That day opened an entirely new world to me. Together, we explored music, laughter, a first kiss, and the following summer he became my first lover.

When Marcus finished playing, I asked him about his music, favorite musicians, songs, and so on. Like Steven, his voice had a gentle softness, and he spoke choosing his words carefully. Once he relaxed, we discovered we had very similar musical tastes. Since the school year was near its end, I asked about his summer plans. He told me he would be working at a local garden shop. I mentioned I was growing tomatoes for the first time and my plants had established buds and looked ready to flower.

When I asked if he planned to pursue music following graduation, he said his parents wanted him to major in something practical, like accounting. Not wanting to contradict his parents, I only said it was important for a person to do what brought them happiness. Then, realizing it had gotten late, I gathered my things, thanked him for sharing his songs with me, and left.

Though I didn't recall having seen him around school before that day, now I saw him constantly, and it always stirred up memories. Before Steven, I'd never known anyone who was Cuban. The other kids would ask him questions about Puerto Rico. I'd say to him, "Why don't you tell them you're Cuban, not Puerto Rican," but he'd only shrug. In our racially homogenous town, him being Cuban and my being Jewish made us both misfits.

The day I went to the Garden Center, I was looking to buy fertilizer for my tomato plants. For weeks, bees had been hovering and going from flower to flower pollinating my plants. Now their first small fruits had appeared and only time and nurturing would help them reach full maturity.

When I chanced upon Marcus, he was restocking a shelf. I asked where I could find tomato plant fertilizer and he led me to an aisle where he picked up a small white bag. As he handed it to me, it slipped through my grasp and fell to the floor. Without a word, he picked up the bag and laid it in my palm, cradling my hand in his. I quickly asked if he'd decided on his major and he told me he intended to enter college 'undeclared.'

Fertilizer in hand, I headed to the cashier, when I thought I heard him call me. He asked if I'd been to the nearby beach, adding it was about forty minutes away. Though tempted, I hesitated. Relocating after my mother's hospice ordeal ended, a new town, a new job, a new school, the changes had kept me busy, but that was all they'd done. So, I set my concerns aside.

Him

She came out of the house wearing a bright orange dress. As she walked to the car, the sun behind her revealed the full shape of her body.

It was hot at the beach. She spread out a blanket, sat for a few minutes, then stood up, took off her dress, and ran down to the water. As a wave approached, she dove in, disappearing. When she didn't immediately surface, I got concerned. But then her head pop up above the water, a good distance from where she'd disappeared. She swam out into deeper water. It was obvious she was a great swimmer, and after doing a bunch of different strokes, she made her way back to shore.

As she walked toward me in her clinging sleek black swimsuit, I could see how well-toned her body was. I yanked off my t-shirt and stretched it across my lap.

"You're a really good swimmer," I said as she bent down and grabbed a towel.

"The Y," she replied. "Aren't you going in?" She shook her head, spraying me with water.

I snatched up my t-shirt, holding it between us.

After that day, I'd stop by her house just to hang out. She had an old piano. Besides music, she knew a lot about books. She lent me a few of her favorites, and after I read each one, we'd discuss it. There were lots of hot sweaty summer nights. When I couldn't sleep, I'd drive by her house, wondering if she was awake, like me.

On one afternoon, when we were checking out her tomato plants, she picked a large ripe tomato and took a bite. As she chewed, its juice dribbled down to her chin. She wiped at it with the back of her wrist, then offered the tomato to me. I stared at her for a moment before taking it. When I bit into it, it tasted so sweet, I closed my eyes. When I reopened them, she was smiling. Then, with her thumb, she slowly wiped away the juice gathered in the corner of my lips.

Since I'd been thinking about asking her to go to the amusement park with me, I chose that moment, and she said yes. The rest of the week I kept thinking about her—in her swimsuit, laughing at my jokes and listening whenever we talked as if my thoughts mattered.

Her

I hadn't expected him to arrive so early. But when I saw him pull up in front of my house, I grabbed the picnic basket and blanket I'd set next to the front door. When we got to the beach, he helped me spread out the blanket, and we both stretched out on it. As we lay there enjoying the warmth of the sun on our bodies, I noticed him sneaking a peek at me every once in a while. There was something sweet about that. I hadn't received that kind of attention in a while.

The sun's rays reflected off the water, making it sparkle. It was so beautiful I couldn't wait to feel it against my skin, so I stood up and removed my sundress.

"You coming?"

"Later," he said, squinting and shading his eyes as he looked up at me.

As I waded out, I felt the sand beneath my feet slipping away with each waves retreat from the shore. When I'd gone far enough out that the water was covering the top of my thighs, I dove in. Memories poured into me and flowed through every inch of my body. Absolute paradise. Having once been a competitive swimmer, I switched between the different strokes I used to practice.

When I returned to the beach, Marcus was still in the same spot. He'd removed his T-shirt, revealing a lean musculature.

"The water's nice," I said, stepping onto the blanket. "You should go in."

"Nah," he replied.

"Please tell me you're not one of those people who goes to the beach and doesn't go in the water." I shook my head, showering him with water from my hair, and left him grasping air, as I leapt out of reach.

That afternoon, we ate lunch in silence, our eyes sometimes meeting and speaking a language all their own. At one point, he asked me where I'd learned to swim. I told him my parents couldn't swim, so they'd insisted I take lessons at the Y.

We relaxed, discussed music, high school, college, and the progress of my tomato plants, which were so laden with fruit their stalks had bent under their burden.

As the sun sank and the tide crept in, we packed up our things. Despite having had misgivings, I felt okay about having gone to the beach with him. When we got back to my house, we sat in the car without speaking. Then, as I reached into the rear seat to get the picnic basket and blanket, he asked if I'd had a good time.

What could I say? That I'd enjoyed spending the day with him? That for the first time in a long while I hadn't felt lonely?

Over summer's remaining weeks, he'd stop by to talk. Sometimes we'd talk about college. Others his parents. There was an old piano in the house I was renting, and the first time he noticed it, he walked over, opened the lid to the keyboard, and began playing. Listening to him play was like soaring upward, the sounds he drew from the piano expressing the thoughts, colors, and flavors of every conceivable human emotion. When the music stopped, it was like experiencing a sudden breathtaking free fall through the sky toward earth.

During some of his visits, we'd go look at the tomato plants. They'd continued growing throughout the summer, and their fruit was turning a deep, full-bodied red. One day, I picked a tomato that looked about to burst. I bit into it, and pure lusciousness filled my mouth and danced across my tongue. I handed the tomato to Marcus, and he took a bite. The look of pleasure on his face will stay with me forever.

He invited me to go with him to the amusement park. I said yes. Not long after that, he left, leaving me alone with memories, guilt, and doubts.

Years earlier, with tears gathering in my eyes, I'd just hung up the phone, when my mother asked who had called. When I told her, "Steven," she said, "Rebecca, I can see you and Steven are getting close. But you should be careful."

"Why?" I snapped.

"Don't misunderstand. He's a wonderful boy. Polite, serious, and hard-working, but he is not for you."

"Why not? Because he's Puerto Rican."

"Pshaw. You know your father and I have always abhorred any kind of prejudice."

"Then what? He's not Jewish? If Dad hadn't been Jewish, you wouldn't have married him? My God, World War II's been over for forever."

"Yes, Rebecca, the war ended. But there's nothing that prevents another madman from spewing lies and distorting reality for his own malevolent purposes and people choosing to believe his lies, and ignore what they know to be the truth."

"But—"

"Accepting reality and truth can be uncomfortable, but it's important. Part of that for you is never forgetting that six million Jews, generations of innocent people were murdered, all because of lies."

"But you and Dad loved each other. When he died—"

"When your father died, I lost my best friend. But, when we married? Well, I knew he was kind and would be a good provider. It was my duty, my obligation to honor those six million people who were slaughtered by preserving our existence, our heritage. That came first. Love came later."

"Then, you'll be happy to know, he's leaving," I shouted, tears streaming down my face. "Steven's father received a promotion, and he's moving away."

Him

We got to the park around mid-morning and made a beeline to the roller coaster. It took some serious convincing, but she finally agreed to ride. She looked absolutely terrorized as we climbed uphill. When we went into our first nose dive, she screamed and grabbed my hand. I tried getting her to ride again, but there was no way. So, I rode the second time alone, by myself. While the coaster climbed, increasing the distance between us, I never took my eyes off her.

Her

Once again, on the Saturday we were going to the amusement park, he arrived early. This time I was waiting. During the thirty-minute drive, he asked about the tomato plants. I told him the last tomatoes had ripened.

After we parked, he led me straight to the roller coaster. I wasn't a big fan of their stomach-flipping gyrations, so I told him I'd wait for him. He grabbed me by the hands, pleading, so not wanting to attract attention, I agreed.

Once we settled in our car with the safety bar lowered and locked in place, I began feeling queasy. It seemed like it took forever for the coaster crawl up the track, each click and clack of its wheels on the rails making my heart beat faster. When we reached the top, we hesitated, then tipped over, and dove straight down with a deafening roar. At the bottom of the hill, the coaster slashed right, before whipping through a series of directional changes at breakneck speed. When we were back at the starting point, Marcus said he wanted to ride again. Since tempting fate a second time was certain to be a mistake, I declined and watched him go on alone.

Later that evening, I bought a paper cone wrapped in pink cotton candy, and he bought a humongous slab of fried dough covered with powdered sugar. When I bit off a piece of the fluffy treat, sugar at that spot melted and hardened into a blood red crust, like a scab covering a wound. He burst out laughing at the thin trail of fluff hanging from my lips.

"You should see yourself," I said, pointing at the powdered sugar he'd sprayed all over his polo shirt.

Though we tried to brush the specks away, they only wedged deeper into the fabric.

"I think it's ending," she said. "We should find the car."

"I'll write," he said. "And you'll write back. Won't you?"

"Summer's ending," she said. "You'll be leaving for college in a few days, and I'll return to teaching English at the high school."

She turned her face away and stared straight ahead. She saw herself as she'd been that morning, closing the lid to the piano's keyboard while a single tear crept down her cheek until it touched her lips, like a kiss goodbye.

In the Dungeon

Dallas Hunter

He led me through the sex dungeon, dressed in his three-piece suit, talking as if he was aggravated he had to be the tour guide.

"This isn't a theme park, there are going to be situations you are presented with that you won't find charming, but it doesn't really matter how you feel about it, the customer is the most important person in the room, got it?"

I nodded at him and adjusted the ties of my two French braids. The hallways were dark, but there were windows into every room from which light illuminated every sexual fetish scenario I could think of, and some I couldn't.

This man, the one who owned the sex dungeon, Theo, checked his watch. We stopped just outside a room that was illuminated. It was a small kitchen and living room combo, and from just a glance it seemed rather in disarray. There was a small French maid costume that he handed me from a hanger on the doorknob.

"Put this on, if it doesn't fit—well you won't be wearing it for long enough to care," he said. I took the outfit from him, and he walked down the hall without giving me a second glance. I smiled just a little, I was finally here.

I got into the room and changed out of my clothes quickly, putting the outfit on and storing my street clothes in one of the cupboards. A small piece of paper in the pocket of the costume told me that this was a role-play scenario in which the client wished to watch me clean, and I was to continue cleaning, despite his every advance, this was his desire.

I had been on the streets for quite some time before this adventure, and I wasn't used to such a novelty. The dungeon offered someone like me so much more than simple alleyway sex or opium den ménage à trois. I had something of a sickness, a need, a deep and haunting desire to be filled and complete, to use and to be used by others. It was insatiable, and it was only a matter of time before I ended up here. Now that I was here, it was a little overwhelming.

As soon as I heard the doorknob, my heart moved into my throat, and I could hear it beating below my jaw. *This is it.* My body flushed, and I could feel the warmth of it spreading all the way down to my groin. This was finally happening.

The gentleman walked in, it was the only way I could describe him, very tall, short hair and shaved, thin build—even in his face, a narrow kind of man. He was in a gray suit with a pink tie, and he closed the door softly behind him. I had been with so many people, he was really no different. It mattered not, what type they were on the surface. To me, the most interesting thing about a person was what was hidden behind their zippers.

"Hi," I said breathlessly. The look on his face was a bit confusing. A mixture of annoyance and surprise.

"Please don't talk, just clean," he said. *Oh.*

I turned around and found a duster on the countertop. It didn't make much sense to dust when the place was already such a mess. There were papers on the countertop and articles of clothing in the sink. I began depositing these in the laundry, and some things in the trash. Before I knew it, I had completely forgotten about the man in the suit, because this new task just seemed to take precedence.

It felt like he didn't want me when he told me to clean, so that was what I did. Only his chuckle brought me out of my fervor.

I looked over at him, and he was covering his smile with his hand and my face flushed. *What's he laughing at?*

"You don't do this very often, do you?" he asked. Mortification was seeping into my pores from his smile. *How can he tell so easily?* All he asked me to do was clean, and although it wasn't overly sexy to me, this was his world and whatever got his socks off was game. I was totally confused.

He stood up, and I felt that I had done something completely wrong. He was going to leave me now, probably tell the owner how bad I was, and I would get kicked out for sure. Tears came unbidden, how could I have failed so badly on my first attempt?

"Relax, it's not over, no need to get emotional," he said. And I sniffed. *How can he even know what I'm thinking?* It was apparent that this man had way more experience than me and I was now the subject of his ridicule rather than desire.

"I … I'm sorry. This is my first time," I said and could have kicked myself again. What the hell was wrong with me? This was my first gig, not my first time! I sounded like a stupid virgin. "In the dungeon," I said, and literally covered my mouth with my hand. I should have slapped myself with that hand. Not only was I admitting that this was my first time here, but also that I was not a professional whatsoever, and that whatever money he had just spent was being completely wasted on me.

Instead of being a total douche, which is what I expected and deserved, he just smiled at me.

"You're quite lucky I'm your client then, I don't think most of the patrons here would be as understanding as me," he said and took off his jacket. He laid it down softly on the couch. Every motion from him seemed suave and efficient. He was cool in every regard.

He continued, "I remember my first time here, it was a bit overwhelming, all of the employees knew exactly what I wanted before I wanted it, they knew how to take me places I didn't even know existed. They were knowledgeable in ways I … at any rate it felt as though I was being cheated, even though they were giving me more than I had expected or bargained for. That is what you will be someday, but the interesting thing about this place, is that sometimes a pairing like this happens, and I actually get to be the one to teach," he said. "Even though this wasn't my fantasy, I like rolling with the scene."

I bit my lip. This was—he was—nothing like I had thought. Expectations were further in the laundry basket than the random socks, and this man was nice to me.

"Here, let me show you," he said. My breath came out quickly as he took my hand and led me to the kitchen. "The counters are low here you see … so that you can bend over them." He pushed me down slightly, and I could feel my breasts press against the cool granite of the countertops. I could see the couch from my position and how he could have a nice view of my cleavage from this angle.

He wet a washcloth in the sink, and I stayed pressed against the counter while I waited for him.

It was warm when he returned and put my hand on top of it. He put his hand on top of mine and moved it slowly over the counter.

"Don't make your movements too quick, it sends a signal that you don't really want to be here and that you want to get the scene over with as fast as possible. Is that what you want blondie?" he asked.

"No," I said in a huff. I could feel his erection against the thin material of my ass, I was surprised I was able to answer at all.

He stepped away from me, and I felt like a deflated balloon. *How long is this lesson going to continue before he fucks me?*

"There's a stepladder here, be careful climbing up," he said. I gripped the washcloth with silent longing as I climbed up the stepladder and he grabbed my ankle gently. I froze in the position with one leg higher than the other on the rungs. "Bend over and reach as far as you can to wipe the far side of the fridge," he said.

I did so, and I could feel how exposed this made my backside. He had a clear view from the couch, and probably an even better view from right underneath me. I sighed as I rubbed the fridge with my washcloth. I could feel the corner of the freezer against my pelvis, and I reached down further just to feel that corner rub up and down against my clit.

"Mmm, that is very nice, come on down, beautiful," he said, and I felt more like I melted down rather than climbed down like a human being. I was a sex puddle.

"What now?" I asked.

"What else needs cleaning?" he asked. I looked around. The kitchen still needed considerable work, but I thought I would burst before long. I looked in the living room where there were little bits of lint on the carpet.

"I could … vacuum," I said, and he smiled.

"Quite eager to get out of the kitchen, aren't you?" he asked, and his eyes crinkled like he knew exactly what I was thinking again. He had such an unfair advantage.

He left me and pulled a bucket out from under the sink and filled it with dish soap. After that, he turned the water on, and I watched it fill high with suds.

On the sink was a scrubbing brush and he took my washcloth and replaced it with the brush. He set the bucket down on the ground.

"Since you seem so eager to clean the floor, do this one first," he said. I dipped the scrubbing brush into the suds and brought it out. I kneeled down on the floor and scrubbed. "Start over there," he said and pointed to the far wall. I pulled my bucket over and scrubbed. "Legs, just a bit further apart, just like that," he said.

I sighed as I air-humped and scrubbed the floor. "Get your breasts on the ground," he said.

"But it's wet," I said.

"That's okay," he answered. The soapy water bled through the material quickly as I moved against the tile. I never knew that scrubbing a floor could be so completely torturous. I wiped the sweat from my brow, not merely from exertion, but more from holding myself together.

I dumped the bucket over the floor and scrubbed every inch of it madly. When I was done, I threw the brush down roughly. *Now he can fuck me.*

"That's a nice clean floor, come now, didn't you tell me that you wanted to clean the carpets?" he asked.

I couldn't escape the little whine that blew through my nose. He laughed and grabbed my pruned hand and led me to the living room portion.

"Now," he said, "There are too many items in here that you'll need to pick up before you can start vacuuming, but don't just pick them up willy-nilly, you have to be slow, seductive, you know how to do that don't you?" he asked.

"I guess," I said softly. This man wanted seduction from me. He could have gone to a whore house for that, but instead, he went to a dungeon. I groaned as I bent over and picked up the random things on the floor. More clothes, tissue boxes, empty bottles of water, various kinds of dishes.

I pretended I was moving in slow motion as I did this, and every time I bent over to get something, I made sure to show this man my ass, and not one time did he plunge his cock into my exposed sex. I was beginning to worry that he did not intend on fucking me at all. I tried not to believe that, as the prospect was just too horrific to think about.

I ran a hand through my hair when I was finished picking things up off the floor. *Where will he take me? Over the counter? Against the wall? On the freshly-scrubbed linoleum?* I wanted all three, but I didn't want to be picky, even one would do.

"Anything else?" I asked.

"Don't tell me you're not going to vacuum, after all that work?" he asked. I stared at him doggedly. He laughed, "In this house, you finish what you start," he said. I stomped my foot like a child.

"I'm sure you can fuck me while I vacuum, why are you so patient? I've never been with a man so frustratingly patient as you!" I said, near hysterics. He held one finger up to his lips to shush me, and I blanched. I decided I hated him then and looked for the vacuum.

I tried to be seductive in my movements, he told me if I went fast it would look like I didn't want him and I wanted this scene to end. Well, that is exactly what I wanted. I wanted to clean the fucking carpet so that he would have no excuses left, that everything would be clean and he could finally fuck me. That was what I wanted, even though this whole scene was for him. I knew that I was being selfish and I could just as well pay for sex my way if that were how I felt but … we were in this together now.

I turned off the switch to the vacuum and stood right before him. There was nothing else to see but me and the wet maid's outfit that clung to me.

"Take that off," he said, gesturing to my outfit. I all but ripped it off of me and he smiled. "Slower," he whispered as I had it nearly off my face. I groaned as I pulled it inch by inch over my body. It stretched uncomfortably before it came off all at once. I was breathing heavily as I threw it down.

"Come now," he said, "you're making your floor dirty again. Don't make me make you vacuum twice, where does that belong?" he asked. I stared at him incredulously. He wasn't joking, he wanted my wet costume in the dirty laundry basket. I picked it up in a huff and threw it inside with the other laundry.

"Anything else?" I asked, almost yelling. This guy had a fucking problem, I was sex on a stick in front of him, begging to be fucked, and he wanted me to clean some more!

"Well now that you mention it," he said darkly. I sunk to my knees. I never cried, but I was going to cry. *Why is he doing this to me?* "I want you to take the vacuum tool and clean the couch a little. It's just this last thing, I swear, clean the couch, and I will end your torture," he said. He was playing with me.

I crawled dejectedly over to the vacuum and pulled it with me over to the couch. Kneeling before a man, I was used to them unbuttoning their trousers, but he did no such thing, just watched me steadily as I flipped the switch while keeping eye contact with him and taking the tool connected to a hose and rubbing it along the couch fabric. It reminded me of a pair of corduroy overalls I used to have.

I began to clean higher on the couch and in one swift movement he had me over his lap, stroking my lower back and rubbing his hand across my ass. I shivered.

"I didn't say to stop, if you don't clean the couch completely, I'm not going to fuck you. I'm a stickler for perfection," he said.

I moved the tool then, but he kept a hold on me, which meant I had to struggle slightly to reach every corner of the furniture from the center of the couch. When I leaned over to get the back, he had my pussy in his face, smelling, tasting, breathing on me. I screamed with frustration and banged my fist against it, fighting it, fighting him so that I could have him. I moved to the side of the couch, and he kneaded my ass with his fingers, probing slightly, making me jump. I kicked at him, and he grabbed my ankle.

From that angle I could reach the bottom of the couch, underneath it, rubbing with the tool like he rubbed my belly, my thighs, my sex.

I turned off the vacuum switch and maneuvered myself properly on his lap. I could feel his girth from beneath his pants on my labia. All he had to do was unzip.

He ran his hands up and down my body, across my breasts, which were moving with my heaving breath. I had worked hard for this, panting and needy on top of him.

"This is unique for me too, a novelty indeed," he said, "it's the employee's job to seduce the client, but instead here I've made you hot and bothered, begging for it on top of me, after making you clean," he laughed. "It's really something," he said.

"Please," I said and placed my hands on the top of his which were on my warm breasts. "Teach me something else," I said breathlessly.

His eyes darkened with desire. "Alright then," he said and unbuttoned himself. With the sound of his zipper, his cock sprung loose, and he grabbed it. "On your knees now," he said, and I lifted myself off his lap and onto my knees as he aimed his cock right at the cusp of my vagina.

I closed my eyes as he placed his hands on my shoulders and guided me down slowly. I could feel him opening me as his cock slid through, and when there was nowhere left to go, he held me there, pressed against the wall of my sex, then fucked me on the couch, the floor, the carpet, and places I hadn't even thought of.

- 41 -

Quiet Combustion

Arielle Jones

Daniel says, "I have someone I want you to meet."

Daniel's shirt is tucked in, and his tie is done up enough that it might be choking him. He cleans his glasses, and his smile is shy when he sees me watching. He's been introducing me to quite a few people lately. I'm not too good at names, but I'm trying. He holds my hand as we walk to the edge of a scene that's just started. "That's Master Erik," he says, pointing at the Dom in the scene. With a black tank top and neatly tailored black jeans, his smile is gentle, hands loosely clasped behind his back as he paces around the naked sub strung up on a cross. There's another Dom there, similarly dressed, but he doesn't seem to matter too much to the sub, so he doesn't quite matter to me.

She, the sub, is blind-folded but her gaze is following her master, his footsteps, the occasional brush of his shoulder against hers. She shivers and bathes in the lowness of his chuckle.

I'm sure she can tell the two Doms apart, especially when Master Erik pauses his pacing around her to say something right up against her ear. It's got to be filthy, or just the perfect thing she needs to hear. She's nodding so quickly, then he swats her behind like an affectionate coach. From the front, the other Dom walks up and lands a solid open hand smack across both of her breasts. They take turns swathing their palms in sporadic places on her skin. At times lightly, and firmly, too.

Like a charm on a necklace's taut chain, she is strung between them. Only slightly does she slide one way or the other with a tilt of her head or a particularly drawn out moan, until I finally take a breath when she does.

I want to be her, I want to be them.

Daniel's hand is too light on my back as we stand on the outskirts of the scene. These Doms are so synchronized. Not a word is exchanged between them as they touch her. Not from what I can see. Now they've just taken their floggers out from their belt loops at the same time. Once they're out, they don't even flog her. They just slowly drape and pull their floggers over different parts of her body, and she turns blindly to follow the swirling lines of contact.

To me she looks like Eve, like Eve meeting the serpent, its cool belly moving across her thighs. The serpent's flickering tongue like the ghosting of their fingertips moving along the sides of her neck and the tops of her kneecaps.

Daniel might not even realize the way his thumbnail serpentines its way between every other vertebra on my back.

I step in closer to him, leaning back a little hoping he'll press harder.

"I went to a class of his on flogging," he says respectfully quiet. I bet Daniel could teach a course on rope-work if he really wanted to. Daniel goes on whispering, "His technique is great."

I hum in agreement, not because I have much experience flogging anyone, but I agree because of what I see happening to her. The way she's responding, how the ends of the leather can deliberately be made to feel like rain or a hot rake.

We watch them edge her into standing on the tips of her toes. We watch Daniel's friend flog her in figure eights in the same spot for a minute straight while the other Dom is audibly smacking the back of his hand against her flinching stomach. "See how he's avoiding her diaphragm? They know their stuff."

When Daniel says diaphragm it's like that word doesn't belong to science, to biology, anymore. I can't remember the last time I heard that word, and it makes my breath catch like I fell out of a swing, like he's putting weight on my lungs, easing out all the air before I can do anything about it.

I must've been quiet, or a certain kind of quiet, because he looks at me, he is so close his gaze goes from one eye to the other in the dark light of the dungeon. He then looks back to the lit-up scene, and I do too, and his hand goes tight around my waist. I lay my head on his shoulder as we watch for a few more minutes.

Daniel and I get water and snacks after he's made eye contact with his friend, Master Erik, who waved us goodbye with a smile, flogger in hand. As Daniel and I sit in the dining area, we don't say much, but our legs make a straight line with how closely they press together, side by side. I eat and chat with passersby as he laughs loudly and invites people to sit with us. And I get it, it's probably good that they're here. We need sentient distractions. We're restlessly trying to keep our hands to ourselves, trying to be respectfully social. No scene for us tonight. We'd decided that before we got here. Tonight, we just came to observe that double Dom scene. Daniel was so good about the game plan too. He made sure not to even bring his equipment in case we got tempted.

I'd be fine if life were mostly this. Learning someone, learning to trust, learning to be trustworthy. I hope he knows he's safe with me. Him and his crow's-feet, the beginnings of salt and pepper in his hair, his stretch marks that show themselves on accident while he thinks he's tucked into his sometimes vibrantly pressed button-ups, the scar on his chin that he ridiculously wants me to keep guessing the origins of. Regardless, all of him is safe with me.

In the middle of his conversation with another rope enthusiast, I scratch Daniel's back where he always seems to itch, and he stops talking to mouth his thanks to me.

Master Erik, who I've learned I can just call Erik, shows up in a plain white t-shirt that he hadn't been wearing earlier with his jeans. He had been working hard. His eyes are bright when he shakes my hand, and he gives Daniel's shoulder a squeeze. Up this close, he seems somewhere between mine and Daniel's age. Experienced and still more than able to do something about it.

"How did you like it?" Erik asks looking at us.

"Amazing as always," is what Daniel says, then they both look to me. I swallow to make sure my voice doesn't crack or anything. "It was great seeing you … seeing you work," I say, "Daniel's been praising you on and off the sidelines."

The three of us chuckle politely. So, I suppose that was okay to say. But Erik surprises me when he adds, "Same to you, Tessa. I'm not gonna lie, I've seen some of your scenes and I had to do a double take. How did Daniel get so lucky?"

"It wasn't luck," I cut in, and I'm staring, daring, until he smiles and looks at Daniel.

"I think the three of us, this could definitely work out," he says.

Before we each go our separate ways, we lightly go over what a week from now will look like. A week from now, we will meet up here at the dungeon, and only Daniel or I will strip me down to my underwear, nothing less.

Daniel will bring his own rope to tie me to the St. Andrews cross. We go over what can't happen in the scene on my end, on Daniel's end, and Erik's end. Daniel and I even have a joint condition, kissing will only be between the two of us, to which Erik laughs, says he'd figured as much. Daniel also points out to Erik that my undergarments and where they cover are also off limits. Other than that, what rules of my body and my experience Daniel follow are the same for this other Dom as well.

And then, the three of us literally shake on everything and head out into the night, into the fresh air and fog, and midnight subways, buses, and cars. Back into the world where things are open in a different way, where wants go unprotected because they are acceptable.

When Daniel and I meet up again, it is a couple hours or so before we have to be in the dungeon to meet Erik. We're a block away at this Thai restaurant he's been going to.

"You brought someone!" the hostess greets him and moves us past plenty of open tables. We get seated behind an elaborate screen with a golden crane catching a fish in its glimmering long, smooth, beak. The only one who can find us in this corner we've been tucked away into is the petite waitress, a giggle in her question about our orders. I get a thumbs-up from her after she takes our menus.

"Guess I'm a catch," Daniel says after she leaves, and I scoff, laughing with him instead of telling him that this whole restaurant, staff included, thinks he's going to pay for my meal, thinks that he pays for my everything. Why else would this woman, this young black woman voluntarily be seen out and about with this man, too big for some people, so animated when he talks to her? Why else would they have dinner together downtown in public?

I want to leave, but he likes it here, and the food smells good, even looks great when the plates hit the table. It's kind of a sour taste to be reminded of the fact that judgments run rampant out here. We're supposed to fit their societal expectations, and if not, then we're expected to be less comfortable. I don't want their contexts, their assumptions put on us. Seriously, we're just two people eating.

"It's nice that we're back here," Daniel says, dabbing his napkin at the corner of his mouth.

"Why?" I ask, slicing a carrot at the bottom of my bowl with a spoon. It's covered in spices and too soft to be satisfying when I cut through it.

"Well," Daniel says as I chew, "we get to go over everything at least sort of privately."

He's right. No one can see us unless they look for us.

Hushed and making one another smirk, we talk about the scene. Since there is the new element of having another whole person involved, I agree with his idea of keeping the implements simple and few. Each of the Doms will simply have a flogger, and there will be a riding crop. Other than that, it's bare hands and the rope to tie me up with.

After our early dinner, which I insist we split, it's time to get ready for tonight.

There are certain things I do every time leading up to a scene.

I change out of my street clothes.

I drink water.

I find Daniel since he's likely being a social butterfly.

I stretch, head to toe.

I initiate intentional small talk with my Dom.

Lastly, we review what to expect in the scene, if there are any changes and why.

Then the three of us meet up at the next available St. Andrew's cross. Daniel wipes it down, and Erik lets me lean on him when I take off my heels. He has the faintest callouses right there at the tops of his palm while he politely holds my elbow. I thank him and set my shoes to the side, and Daniel pecks my shoulder, says to our group that we're all set.

Erik has his own way of getting into a scene. He has all three of us hug, with me in the middle. It's different than what I'm used to. I feel blocked even from the ceiling lights and from the view of everyone else. Daniel's cheek is on one of mine and Erik's is on the other. Daniel has some stubble I hadn't seen, but I can feel it, familiar and gently rough. The other Dom's cheek feels so smooth. I almost pull away when it moves, when he begins to talk as we stay huddled together.

To no one specific he shares how grateful he is that he's been welcomed in by us, how he's noticed that I only play with Daniel, so he doesn't take my trust lightly. Daniel rubs my side. We listen to his friend complimenting my caution, my care, how I'm the first sub in a good while to ask him what he needs for aftercare before he's had to bring it up. He goes on to say humidly in our little human tent how willing he is to be an instrument tonight in this scene.

It all sounds so much like a prayer, especially when he says at the end, "May this scene be everything we hope for it to be, but may it also delight us however it may."

We all take a step away from each other then, and I blink my eyes, not knowing I had closed them.

Daniel steps behind me and unzips my dress like it's nothing but in his way. I thought I'd be able to watch Erik watching me, but instead, I look safely just past his ear. A couple people take seats nearby and angle them to see us better. I haven't seen them here before. My back straightens, and my chin lifts, and Erik is smiling at me. Daniel's hand on my calf steadies me, the touch also tells me to step back, to move closer to the cross to lean against it. The tan rope, as he coils it around the bottom of my shin, feels like his stubble, comforting. I keep my head up and facing the crowd, facing Erik, but my mind is with the loops and knots Daniel is making. He tugs here and there, slips two fingers between the rope and my skin to be sure nothing is too tight or too loose. His knuckles feel nice, feel casual like the skin to skin contact is almost by accident.

"Do you want to see?" He asks, knelt before me, looking up at me where some people think Doms aren't supposed to be.

I hope his knees are okay as I nod.

His smile is permission, so I look down my leg.

The knots make a zigzagging braid from my ankle to just below my calf. It's beautiful and symmetrical, and each loop around is evenly spaced. It almost looks like a more elaborate version of the legs of a gladiator's sandal. And I feel that way, ready for battle.

"I'm going to do the other one, okay? Can Erik help me?"

The other Dom doesn't move forward until I agree, and even then he only helps by feeding out rope to Daniel as he laces up my other leg. He's just as careful as he was with the first one and each tug of his to adjust the knots sinks me deeper. He was so right when we first met, this is like meditation.

Across the way, I see more people than there were before, but I'm not at a place where I can count, where counting interests me.

"Open," Daniel says, and on autopilot, I widen my legs, and he ties each of them to the bottom legs of the wooden X I lean against. After he finishes that he brings himself up to eye level with me and my mouth opens, ready for his.

Then comes the gentlest rejection as he tips shut my jaw with two confident fingers under my chin. He turns me into a gaping pond fish denied breadcrumbs. I think of that vivid wide-eyed fish caught in the mouth of the crane from the Thai restaurant, all bewildered and clumsy with its mouth open for no reason. I flood hot in my cheeks, and the heat spreads out to my ears and down my neck.

"I have to do your arms," he tells me. I swallow and look down because I know that. Legs, then arms, then he'll kiss me, right? We didn't say so, but I hope that's what he means. That's how it usually goes.

At my periphery, just past Daniel's concentrate-ing face, is Erik running his fingers through his flogger. The leather drips from his fingertips and softly patters together as it gathers together again. He looks ready, looks at my body like he's deciding where to start to take me apart. I think of that woman from last week, of her face when she'd felt the very same flogger relentlessly striking her in the same place for so long. He'll get my calves, maybe? Did Daniel leave my calves open on purpose? Could either of the Doms even reach my calves with the wood in the way? But that's not for me to worry about. I can't figure that out for them right now, not while my arms are getting so considerately tied open, stretched out over my head.

It's a conscious thing when I tell myself to relax. I trust in the rope, in my legs, in the fact that Daniel wouldn't let me fall, even if the ropes somehow did. I do that thing where you force your body to relax to help your mind do the same, and my body then warns me.

Urgency happens between my legs, it terrible and, fuck, he's worked so hard, and I don't want to ruin it. Then again, there's also that fact that watersports aren't quite for my Dom and me. I clench quickly and get those icy prickles even though I've caught myself in time.

My arms and legs are securely tied and Erik steps close to me, flogger held low but ready. Daniel takes one look at my face and literally grabs the other man's wrist and says, "Yellow," with a glare and I'd almost be scared of him if I didn't know he was worried about me.

Oh God, he thinks it's something serious.

When he asks, "What's wrong?" it's low and with both hands cupping my face in a way that's somehow not overdramatic, but just concern, just care. Cupped in his hands like the delicate face of a rose, I'm glad he's close enough for me to whisper when I say, "I um, I think I have to go to the bathroom."

A blink, a frown, and then he just laughs, "Are you serious right now?"

Behind him, Erik lowers the safety shears he'd picked up at some point while Daniel had been checking on me.

"No, but are you serious?" Daniel says, and it's part disbelieving, part entertained, and part sweetly exasperated because honestly, that had to be at least half an hour of ropework he'd put in. With a wince and an embarrassed nod from me, he 'scolds' me for making him worry with a hard close-mouthed kiss, then he starts the unraveling process.

He's in the middle of laughing to himself when one of my arms get free, and I rub his chest, feel the rumble of his laugh, and he shakes his head at me.

His, "Jesus, Tess," is warm as he stops what he's doing to kiss my free hand. He already knows, but I tell him I'm sorry.

My cheeks hurt from smiling when he scoffs. Daniel hardly scoffs. He starts to free my legs but says, "Please tell me you saw it?"

I already know he means his work, the patterns of the rope, his beloved hemp braids he'd devoted to me. I nod, and when I'm completely free I hug him, and he swats my butt as I actually giggle and scurry off to the bathroom to the sound of Daniel explaining to Erik that I just had to step out to the ladies' room. I run back just to slip on my shoes, then I'm off again.

He may have called it the ladies' room, but really, it's just the single restroom with three stalls and a cleaning station. I try to make things quick, misguidedly hoping that somehow if I'm fast enough, we can slip back into our mental spaces like nothing happened. I puff out a laugh to myself, and it echoes as I think of the sharp, playful, glint that had been in Daniel's eyes as he'd released me. I'm in trouble when I get back, the good kind.

I flush, wash my hands, and take a few deep breaths at the sink. Some of the words from Erik's BDSM prayer wander back into my head.

Let me be an instrument.

Back at the cross, I toe off my heels, and the two men finish their small talk. There in my underwear with hands smelling like watered down lavender, I apologize to Erik who smiles and shrugs with an 'it happens' vibe. Next, I go to apologize to Daniel, and he raises a brow, pulls his hand away when I reach for it. He's quick though to hold the side of my neck, to pull me into a hug. I hug him back, put my toes on the coolness of his dress shoes.

"Back to the cross?" I ask, but he shakes his head.

"New plan," he says, "there's a punishment for wasting my work." He winks at me though to soften the unfelt accusation. The new plan ends up being for me to hold my arms up on my own, no ropes. He'll give me breaks, rub my muscles when I need it, and will let me lay my arms on his shoulders if I need to. The new plan is agreeable to all of us, so we go with it.

I lean back on the St. Andrew's cross again and notice it's a little cooled down since my absence. I hold on as comfortably high as possible to the outstretched arms of the cross and wait for my Dom and his friend to approve. A *Vitruvian Woman*, but not so stoic. I display myself and trust that I'm the best specimen I need to be for them.

"Well look at you," and it's Daniel talking but so recognizably in control. We did get back so quickly. I don't know how I doubted that he could get us back to this space. He's so good at this, so good for me. He rubs my thighs one at a time as if I'm cold. We hardly do spankings on my legs, but that's what happens. He starts slow, warms me up, talks me up, tells me what I look like before he slaps the meatiest parts of my legs, no rhyme or reason to it that I can concentrate on.

My eyes are closed to keep me from guessing his pattern. I can feel my flesh jiggle as the force gets harder, and the self-consciousness takes a little time to go away as he keeps it up. I'm stinging in enough places eventually that it becomes an overall burn. I flinch sometimes, and it feels like he doesn't care the way he rakes his nail down my hips, starting from the bottom-most lace of my underwear and scraping down to the tendons of the tops of my feet.

I suck in air as quietly as I can. We just started, but he makes it feel the way the spanking bench feels after an entire scene. I have too much skin, my legs are too long, he's found too much of me already. I have to adjust my grip on the cross and right then is when the drizzling tips of the flogger rain softly from the crown of my head to tickle my cleavage, and an edge of one of the strips of leather catches at my bellybutton. I hum so I don't moan. I'd forgotten that there are four hands tonight, not just Daniel's.

Daniel's hands rub everywhere he's struck me with his palms, and it doesn't feel like it did before, like being warmed from the cold. This time it feels like that metal thing, that thing in some people's kitchens that scrape the colored skin off of apples. Even after the top layer faintly browns, there's more to scrape away to brighten nearer the core. There's nowhere to hide. I fidget my footing, and my lungs can't get full enough, but I keep my grip because I said I would, because he said he'd wanted me to. *Apple peeler*—that's what it's called.

The flogger lightly tests my wrists. It makes wind like the beating of bird wings, just privately moving air enough for only the small to feel. Then the flogger hits back and forth over my arms, careful to avoid my head and it actually feels like feathered wings, like I'm trying to reach up to catch something that wants to fly away.

The sharp hit to my hip tells me that I've started rolling my hips, so I stop, and Daniel presses his mouth to my quivering stomach. It's his mouth. It has to be. It better be. Then he nips at me below the underwire of my bra, and I know. He licks a swipe down the side of my rib, a damp paintbrush, swift and soft and soothing.

Like lightning, he brings down both hands hard on the tops of my thighs, and I yell, and he does it again, and he yells at me to open my legs. I do, I stand at attention, my arms burning no matter how obliging the flogger is trying to be to me.

"Get her legs."

The flogger smatters on my bare legs without pause.

My eyes open and Daniel isn't far, and I can tell that when he spoke to Erik, he'd been watching me. I can't prove it, but the idea has my stomach flipping and twisting into something squirming. I close my eyes again. He's too sharp, too bright in the cheeks and the gleam in his eyes.

He kisses me where all I can do is surrender. It's crooked because of how he has to stand out of the way for my legs to continue getting hit, and it has teeth and fire and knows me too well. I have to moan, and it comes out loud, makes our teeth vibrate in little clicks off each other. He leans into me, and his slacks burn the side of my leg just by brushing it, brushing the velvet of my nerves in the wrong direction.

He isn't talking to me when he talks to my lips, hot breath and no hands on me, "Pass me the crop."

I can't do the crop, I can barely do this. The crop is always accurate, always fierce, only soft before it strikes. And true to that Daniel's only warning to me is one pass of the head of the crop down my side.

It finds me hard and quick on my bicep, muscles already aching me in waves of charring effort.

The flogging is still happening, is a constant pain like running too fast through summer grass, the tips of the green blades whipping over skin young, and open, and soft-tender. It itches. I bring my legs a little closer together, then correct myself, but I've already been seen. The flogging comes harder, the riding crop hits my other arm, and my fingers twitch.

"See that," Daniel says quietly, but we all know I can hear him, "see she won't let go. She's too stubborn." He sounds so proud of me. I tell my arms they aren't tired, tell my knuckles they aren't stiff, that if he says so, that I can do more. He's only asked this one thing of me, to hold on, so I can hold on.

The flogging slows, I hear them whisper, then Daniel tells him, "Go ahead."

Layers of leather swipe down my entire front and my head gets pulled back by my hair. This is the part where the executioner would come in, where the blade would find a perfect line. Only by the scrape of familiar lazy shapes on my scalp do I know it's him there, Daniel. But the flogger, the flogger just gets louder between my legs, and I twist in my own grip because he's found me, and it isn't Daniel because Daniel must be behind me.

"Not down," Daniel says, near to where I thought he'd be, "bring the strokes up. Yeah, see. See her feet."

I uncurl my toes, but I'm thrumming, have noise being reeled out from low inside me. I have to be bleeding. The air feels too sharp on me. Where is my skin? My nerves are too close to everything. He's got to keep me, please keep me together. I'm like that pilot.

When I was little, a plane crashed in the neighborhood field, there was no fence. Us kids would play tag or catch or just run. But that day, we'd all come just to watch the fire. The plane had been red, a single seater, wing bent wrong and fire all in the cockpit and glowing through the gaps of the propeller on the nose. All our little voices, and all our little questions, and no one could say they'd seen an ambulance come. It was too hot to get close enough to squint and see if anyone was in there, but I tried. The fire felt dangerous, and like it cared nothing about the man, made me wonder why God had chosen a flood and not this instead. This was a roar and crackle and cared about no one. No one could be alive in there. No one.

This is what that cockpit had to feel like, crashing toward the ground and forgetting the fearlessness of flight.

"You're shaking," Daniel says with his nose pressed against the side of my face, against the smudged airplane window.

I whine. If I talk, I'll cry. I told myself I'd only cry here with him, only him. We aren't alone.

"Talk to me," he beckons, calm and right there in my ear, closer than the sound of the flogging thudding upwards getting me tingling heavily.

"It's too much," I gasp out.

"If it really is then you need to say your word."

I twist, shoulder blades bumping the wood in fits.

The flogging pauses and without looking I know it's because Daniel made it stop.

"Green, I'm good, I'm good," I say in a rush, I don't want this taken from me because he's being protective.

"Okay, turn around," says my Dom. I do as he says.

It's two floggers now, it has to be. My arms are numb as I grab lower down on the cross, but my back, where I can feel all of it. The figure eights don't stay slow for long. One of them starts just below my neck, and the other comes up from the heels of my feet. I arch into and away from the blows. They rotate space, they find new skin, more skin than I should have, they find it all. My underwear seems pointless except to remind me where I can be touched by only Daniel, but he hasn't yet. But I've been good, I know I have, he even said so earlier, I think. I can't remember the exact words, but he'd praised me. I always do what he says, I'm always listening, I pay attention, to all he asks from me, and to what I give him, what I make sure to give him. *Why won't he touch me?*

I plead in wordless ways, sometimes sounding like I'm on the verge of stamping my feet. Sometimes sounding like I'd dare either of them to ever switch places with me. I'm good, I'm being good, as good as I can be.

"Dan please!" I sob out before I can help it. One of them has been gashing me in the same spot one time too many, or maybe one flog away from one too many.

He curses behind me, grabs my shoulder and spins me around. It's like rug burn the way the wood chafes my inner arms, so used to holding on that the suddenness of my turning feels like me tearing away from myself. I fix my posture as soon as I can but it's hard on my shaky legs, knees having been locked, and my arms feel dead and if I raise them I'll—

"Look at me," he says it and my eyes open without having to think about it, without wondering if he's talking to me.

He's blurry, and I keep blinking, blink as fast as I can because I can't do anything with my hands just yet. I don't know if they can move, if they're even there at the ends of my wrists.

He wipes my eyes for me, and my thanks to him are wet and halfway clogged in my throat. Over and over he swipes his thumb through the wetness of my lashes, dipping warm oars into the water, and I keep making new tears when I'm too hot to have water inside me. It doesn't make sense.

"Hold on," he says, "hold on, you're doing so well."

"Take me to the couch," I tell him as he swipes snot away from between my lip and my nose, "lay me down."

I get wrapped in a blanket, I get laid down and pet in mundane places like the tops of my shoulders and my covered shins until I can stop sniffling, until he can pour juice into my mouth without worrying about me choking. I can't tell what fruit I'm tasting. He's cradling me. I don't even remember walking to get here. To the quiet room with the couches that I know. That I know, I know.

"We carried you over," he says as I lay on his chest.

I don't remember asking him. I don't remember saying goodnight and thank you to Erik, but Daniel promises that I did, so I must have. I'm still so shaky, I haven't been this shaky this long. It almost feels like being dehydrated and having too much adrenaline at the same time. I don't fit quite right in all this space between my fingertips and my spine.

Is this a drop? Am I seriously dropping right now? But that was so good, the scene. It was what I wanted.

When I squeeze the damp material on Daniel's chest, when I crush it slowly, that's when he holds me closest. He's solid, he's solid for us until I can get myself together. I'm not breathing hard anymore, sweat should be drying. My legs are draped over his slacks, and his chin is on my forehead. He should almost shave. I kiss his neck though because it's there and salty warm. I like that chuckle on his lips. It's relieved.

I'm okay, just floating longer than I'd expected. I tell him so in a whisper and a relieved laugh of my own. Things start to cool down like normal after that. He holds me, I lean into him, he tells me the short list of things he might do tomorrow, and I love listening to that. With my ear against his slick shirt, it sounds like I'm eavesdropping on someone a room away who doesn't mind that I'm eaves-dropping. Like he'd be on the phone and peek around the corner with a wink and just keep on talking because he knows I don't mind and that I wouldn't even want to rush him.

I know it's time to go because I think I may have dozed off for a second there. Daniel brings me more water before he brings me the clothes I want to change into for the bus ride home. He takes off his sweaty button up and rolls it up into a plastic bag to keep separate from his other things. His undershirt is no better, but he shrugs when I point that out, says that's what happens after a good nights' work. *Yeah,* I roll my eyes when I get up. *This dork.*

Serious when he wants to be, but definitely a passionate dork. And considerate, and so I ask him something when we get to the breezy midnight sidewalk where no one will have any idea what we're talking about. "Daniel, how did you know when to say 'yellow?' I mean, how did you know I actually needed something?"

I have a beanie on now, and pants and a sweater and a scarf. I can ask him this now.

His pause is short as he readjusts his duffle at his side, he says, "I know you now, I think."

I go with the urge and give a quick kiss on his shoulder. Since we're walking, it makes me accidentally dent the inside of my lip with my teeth. Once I reach my bus stop, our hug is normal as we say goodnight and promise to check in on one another. But for the whole bus ride, at nearly every other misty stoplight, I run my tongue along the inside of my mouth to still feel the wet texture of his shirt.

Survival Tactics

C.W. Bigelow

Though it is a relief to get back to the lake cottage, it isn't the same without her. Our summer clothes are still packed in Dad's old Marine trunk. It is tucked away in the attic all year, and a musty scent wafts out when I open it. Sturdy and spacious, it easily holds the separate piles for each of us. Mom meticulously packed it last week. The dark, pock-marked metal trunk, still boasting Dad's name and Marine rank from World War II, has been hauled to the cottage every summer since they purchased it.

If she were here, all the clothes would already be in the respective dressers and the trunk already stored in the closet under the staircase. The summer would be underway—the sleep-in mornings, hours on the beach, tanned skin, novels, swimming, tennis, and golf—but everything is on hold.

"As soon as she gets out of the hospital, we'll make arrangements up here so she'll be comfortable." Deepening dark circles anchor Dad's blue eyes. Between visits to the hospital, keeping up with his workload at the firm, and watching over three kids, the toll is cracking his smooth demeanor. His blank expression is a clue to his confusion and general feeling of helplessness. It frightens me, because I've never known him to be anything but confident.

A pink haze masking the sinking sun on the horizon floats over Lake Michigan like a chiffon drape. The air is still, and crickets call to each other from the woods on both sides of the house. The familiar tinkle of martini ice sings with the magical sound of a music box, but only half as loud because of her absence. Dad's loosened tie appears confining, as though no matter what he does he is caged by this new dilemma. His trembling hands fumble with a cigarette and mumbles beneath his breath as though I'm not here. "Forty years old. What kind of fucking age is that to have a stroke?" He turns to me with a defeated smile. "Who'd of ever thought?"

And with his comments, I'm suddenly thrust into the role of advisor to the man who up until this point has always had the answers. I'm at a loss as to how to react and keep tugging at memories of his lectures when his advice seemed so sagely, but fail to recall anything that might be of use. Fearful of letting him down in his time of need, I bounce nervously, shifting back and forth in the squeaky wicker chair—glancing at the door to the living room, expecting her to waltz in with her own martini. And I realize I am expecting this, and because of it, I am holding my emotions intact; employing survival tactics of fantasy without even realizing it.

The safety of these evenings, the secure feeling of shared acceptance when laughter was exchanged, hanging on their words or them on mine, is now threatened. What was once in our control no longer is, and tense anxiety hovers over us like an approaching thunderstorm.

Dad reaches across the table and gives me a reassuring fist bump, but I recognize the scripted effort and wince. "What an eighteenth-birthday present huh? Sorry, your old man isn't always as strong as he should be."

The confession did little to allay my fears. I understand it is his way of bringing me into the loop and showing respect, but what I want is a suit of armor, the image of the man I knew two weeks before, a friendly, somewhat aloof figure of strength. If he can't provide that, how am I going to get off this merry-go-round?

Mom is an award-winning athlete, who from all appearances is in exemplary physical shape. Tall and blonde, she saunters into a room with the casual ease of someone who knows exactly what she wants with little doubt she'll achieve it. Her chocolate eyes gleam above her straight nose with energy that sees through anything or anyone. Her deep, sultry voice, fuels a laugh that cascades like a musical instrument, melodiously announcing her arrival.

The stroke struck on the tennis court as she drove the net, setting up for a rifle-like overhead smash. Arm cocked, knees bent, back coiled, before she slumped to the floor defenselessly allowing the ball to bounce off her shoulder while the racquet hit the hard court with a clang. On the next court at the Bay Shore Tennis Club, I had just returned a backhand to Greg Jeffrey, the pro. Oddly, Greg ignored my shot and darted through the opening in the transparent curtain that separates courts.

Confused, I watched him run up to her. Her opponent was already on the phone for an ambulance. Greg tried intercepting me as I approached attempting to protect me. She was a dull gray; her mouth listlessly ajar with her tongue limply exposed on her lips.

As the paramedics strapped her onto the gurney, I maneuvered to give them her personal information and had already grabbed her insurance cards from her purse. Though her eyes were shut, mouth still open and limp, a calm washed over me as they wheeled her out. I was used to her competing and succeeding, and convinced myself it was just another competition she would ultimately win.

"Thanks for taking care of things at the club," Dad sighs as he sits down on the wicker couch with another drink. "Greg told me how you took over and directed the paramedics."

"No big deal. I was fine. Kinda thought about what Mom would do in that situation and followed her lead."

My upbringing has been one of careful nurturing, where all questions are answered openly, or the so-called expert openly admits ignorance and the answer is researched as a team. Mom feels hiding the realities of life can only delay maturation and scoffs at those who feel such honesty brings a child along too quickly for their own good. She might be disappointed to see that I'm groping for answers, feeling anything but equipped to deal effectively with this tragedy.

He flops back into the couch with utter exhaustion. "I pick up Karen at the airport tomorrow and bring her up here. Then I'll head back to the city. Your brother and sister will stay with Aunt Kate for a while, till we get things under control. It's too late to rearrange things, and the kids will be up here soon, so we'll just have her come. Okay?" The edge in his voice tells me to forget arguing.

By the time I wake the next morning; Dad is gone. Wandering to the edge of the cliff, staring at the sky curved above the lake, I wonder if Mom is aware of what has happened.

"It gets the blood flowing," she claimed, winking and nodding towards Dad, raising her voice. "I'd skinny dip if your father wasn't such a prude." We smiled, waiting for his response.

Camouflaged by the newspaper, he growled, "I've nothing against it, as long as the neighbors aren't grossed out."

Mom playfully tossed a piece of toast into the shield of the paper.

Mom preaches equality, but not to the point where jokes can't be played, and she prides herself on just being one of the guys—able to dish out shit with the best of them and loves doing so. But, there is always a place for it, and a man should never actually believe he is better than any woman—and if she feels someone is lording it over her or another woman, she will attack, taking great pride in putting the man in his place.

I wander out to meet Dad and Karen upon hearing the car wind around the gravel in the circular drive. "How is she doing?" I call as I turn the corner of the house.

As Karen emerges from the car, I come to a halt. A mystical mist seems to surround everything around her, yet she moves in clear vision.

Her curly blonde hair frames her tanned, square face. Wide-set blue eyes sparkle as she surveys the house with hands on her slender hips. Long legs flow from short, white tennis shorts. The way she moves, each limb in sync—a graceful flow of energy that brings to mind a well-orchestrated ballet.

She gazes at the house. A sprawling white, wooden structure with a sloping green roof, it has six bedrooms and a sleeping porch. Two wings jut out on opposite ends, forming a courtyard in the front. Her bedroom will be in the wing off the kitchen. The rest of us sleep in the opposite wing. Upstairs, atop the belly of the house, two more bedrooms and a sleeping porch with six beds are used for guests.

Karen shakes her head in amazement as Dad introduces me as Danny.

For the first time in my life I have a strong desire to be called Dan, but just nod and stick out my hand.

"I'm sorry about your mom." It doesn't seem to be a quick quip. Concern flows from her eyes as they squint directly into mine.

I glance at Dad, yearning for news. Shocked he hasn't already updated me on what has transpired during the day, I'm met with a blank stare that only fuels my curiosity. *Is it good news? Bad? Or none at all?*

"Show me the lake," she requests, already on her way around the house.

I skip to keep up with her long, purposeful strides.

"Wow!" she laughs when it comes into view. "I can't wait to dive in."

I understand her astonishment, for no matter how many times I have looked over the cliff, it still excites me, but sharing her reaction enhances the panorama of the depths between sandbars—deep green and dangerous—churning into whitecaps as they race to shore.

"Is it cold?" Her eyes widen with anticipation.

"Call it refreshing at this time of the season. It's bearable, but will become very comfortable later in the summer."

"So, we're talking nipple-hard?"

She says it with such ease and lack of pretentiousness that I'm not shocked. "Pretty much. My Mom swims each morning. Get's her blood flowing."

Dad is sipping a martini when we join him on the screened porch. "I put your luggage in your room, which we can show you later. I brought you both Cokes."

"Did you see her?" I interrupt, suddenly recalling the severity of the situation after my short diversion with Karen.

He winces as a sip goes down and turns his attention to me, though he still isn't making direct eye contact. "Let's sit down. Dr. Babson doesn't think we'll know much for a few days." He lights a cigarette.

Karen smiles, taking the cue and pulls a pack of cigarettes from her purse as she grabs a chair across from us.

Dad quickly turns his attention to Karen. "What's your story?"

Gazing at the floor, she smiles. "Well, I'm kind of engaged, or was … it's a little messed up." She drags on her cigarette and doesn't say anything more.

I shift uncomfortably, not sure I want to be hearing about her personal life, not sure it is any of our business.

"Sounds as though there are some doubts?"

"There weren't."

For the first time, I'm seeing the man the way others see him. Quickly transforming from a parent to the charmer Mom always claims him to be, I'm proud and listen in hopes the direction will keep my mind off Mom.

"Doubts never stop. Questions and surprises when you least expect them." He gazes past her at the lake.

She slides to the edge of her chair, long legs extending straight out like antennae of her sexuality, but she assumes the position so casually, it doesn't appear covetous. "My mother is pissed cause he's older than I am. I mean, I'm not a kid."

She shakes her head, sending her waves of cascading curls into a shudder. "She's afraid he'll use me, ya know?"

Dad takes a sip and leans forward, elbows resting on his knees. "How much older?"

"Dwayne's twenty-seven." She adds quickly, "Seven years isn't a lifetime." She pulls another cigarette from her pack and lights it with the old one. Exhaling an impressive cloud of smoke, she falls back into her chair, bouncing her feet. "I gotta admit something to both of you right up front, okay?" Her gaze bounces from Dad to me.

"I didn't want this job. She made me take it. Says it will be good for me to get away, see more of the country before settling down. All that crap, ya know. She just wants me to get the hell away from Dwayne."

Dad is amused by her candor.

"I wasn't going to come. I was going to tell her I was, but take off. I can take care of myself."

"It appears so," Dad agrees.

"I planned to run away with Dwayne."

I want to ask her why she didn't. Just jump in and join the conversation instead of sitting on the sidelines. But I watch Dad, who sits back and crosses his legs without responding. It's obvious he's enjoying the conversation, using it to get his mind away from Mom.

Sitting straight up as though someone poked her, her eyes grow wide and her mouth tenses into a hard line of anger. "I went to his place with my suitcase ... all I own, and a carton of cigarettes. Good to go, ya know." She shuts her eyes for a moment displaying an expression of anger and shock. "Jane Finney answered his damn door! Can you believe it?"

"A friend?" I ask.

"Not any longer. Course, he claims nothing was happening. Maybe not at that moment, but what was she doing there? She wasn't there to send me off, 'cause I hadn't told either of them about my plan." Leaning back, she takes a deep breath, visibly shaken by the memory.

I wake with a start. A cool night breeze raises goosebumps on my bare chest as I sit up. Drawn by the flapping drapes, I climb slowly out of bed and peer across the courtyard. Her bedroom light shines, and her drapes are wide open. A wave of excitement shoots through my belly. Leaning over a suitcase, she is clad only in white panties. Hauling clothes from suitcase to a dresser her firm breasts bounce slightly. I can't lie back down until her light goes out.

Mom is open about nudity. She shows pride in her body, and though she doesn't flaunt it in front of us, she certainly never hides it. My understanding of a woman's anatomy comes solely from seeing Mom emerge from the lake. My understanding of sexual relations also comes from her, who never fails to openly address any curiosity we express and loves to tease me when she catches me stealing second glances at girls—always playfully conducting stringent interviews to any of these girls I date. Because of my admiration for her, I probably listen more closely to her advice than any other eighteen-year-old does to his mother, but haven't found relationships as complicated as she claims.

Awakened at dawn by Dad's car driving away, I rise for a swim in hopes it will clear my mind. I have to escape the gray dawn visions in which I drift from conversations with Mom to visions of Karen. Karen speaks in Mom's voice—promising me all the medical problems will soon be solved.

The lake lazily laps the beach under a hazy sky. I stop at the edge of the cliff at the sight of Karen marching confidently, stark naked, to the water, tight round buttocks lifting and dropping with each step. The correct thing to do would be to turn around and head back to the house, but I freeze as she dives from the shore. From behind the forest, the sun begins to burn off the haze, and I don't move when she emerges and walks across the sand to her towel. My knees buckle when she looks up and waves before wrapping the towel around her. I glare a while longer, amazed by her boldness, before finally retreating to the kitchen.

"I didn't get any calls, did I?" she asks as she bursts through the screen door into the kitchen.

Shaking my head, I find it hard to look directly at her.

"He's an hour ahead of us." She leans into the refrigerator and pulls out a pitcher of orange juice. "Maybe he won't call," she rambles as she pours a glass and downs it in two gulps.

It's obvious she isn't embarrassed which relaxes me, realizing I won't have to offer any excuses for staring.

"Got a girl?" she asks as she tightens her towel above her breasts then leans against the counter. The towel barely covers her, trimmed pubic hairs peeking out. I look away.

"No."

"Probably better off. Love can be the worse damn thing ever." She tilts her head and smiles. "'Course, it can be the best damn thing ever too. Pretty much a no-win situation."

"So, if it's a no-win situation, would you rather be in love or not?"

She moves to the window to look at the lake's horizon, the towel rising up the bottom of her tight buttocks. "Depends. If you ask me when I'm making love, I'm definitely going to tell you I'd rather be in love. Ask me when I'm in a fight, and then I'd rather not be. Since I'm in a fight at the moment, I guess I'd rather not be. Less pain. I gotta shower." Her exit is quick and deliberate, leaving me breathless.

"I won't be home tonight, Danny. I've got to go to the hospital, then stop in and see the kids," Dad explains when he calls from the office.

"How much do they know?"

"Nothing. Do you think I should tell them the truth?"

"You're going to have to soon. Billy is old enough to know. I don't know about Cindy. But the problem becomes keeping Billy from telling Cindy. I doubt he'll be able to explain it, so in the end, it's probably better to keep it from them until she gets home."

Dad chuckles. "Where was I when you grew up?"

"Keeping Mom from skinny dipping."

Dad gulps hard and holds back a sob. "I'll call you later, okay?"

"I'll be waiting. Tell her I love her."

After her shower, Karen pops bread into the toaster without any comment. Her sudden moodiness catches me off guard. The phone rings and I grab it without thinking. It's a wrong number, but I'm taken aback when she snaps, "Let me get the damn thing from now on."

It's as though I've been stung by a bee. "It wasn't him, okay!" I yell, leave the house, and fly down the steps to the beach. Sitting at the water's edge, rocking back and forth, I finally let tears fall as I watch the waves roll into shore. Gazing up the shoreline conjures visions of Mom jogging, before being replaced by the ambulance pulling away under a flashing red light and the whine of its sirens. The tears clear my view of the incident, putting it into a new perspective, enabling me to understand how dire the situation is, as I recall the hopelessness of Dad's rambling and his avoidance of my questions. As I stand, hypnotically watching the waves roll in, I wonder when or if I'll ever speak with her again.

"I'm sorry I snapped at you," Karen apologizes upon my return. She winces at my red eyes. "You have a hell of a lot bigger problems to worry about than I do, and I shit on you cause some no good is treating me like he always does. Doesn't say much for my character." She lights a cigarette.

I grab a chair across the kitchen table from her and rub my eyes.

"Must have been a shock?"

"She's never been sick before ..."

"Forty?"

I nod.

She stares curiously for a moment. "She must be quite beautiful."

"Why do you say that?"

"Your father's a great looking guy. He wouldn't marry some dog. Since you don't look like your dad, you must look like her."

"Everyone says I look like her, especially in the eyes. 'Course she always tells me looks aren't everything."

Karen laughs. "They ain't if you got them. Believe me, if you don't have them, they become more important. I'm told I look like my old man."

"Do you think so?"

"I've only seen a picture of him." She leans back and folds her arms across her breasts. "He died in a car wreck coming home from the hospital the night I was born. I guess he saw me in the nursery, but he never did get a chance to hold me." Her voice trails off. "We've always been on our own. My mother has never even dated another man. Drives me crazy. She smothers the hell out of me."

"I can't imagine never having a father."

"My shrink says that's why I'm man crazy."

"Do you agree?"

"No more than any of my friends. Sex is great with the right person. Nothing wrong with that. What's wrong is my mother not dating. He's gone for good. Ain't coming back. I just don't understand her. Sometimes I think she's jealous of me and my ability to find love."

"With Dwayne? Jealous of Dwayne?"

"Of me. Of my happiness." She pauses as she lights another cigarette. She appears confused. "But what do I know? I used to think I had all the answers until I walked in on my best friend and my boyfriend."

"But nothing was going on."

"That was for your father's benefit. I have my own key to his place. They were doing it on the kitchen table!" Tears quickly puddle. "I don't know who to hate more. My mom says I'm attracted to the shits of the world." She gazes out the window for a moment. "She may be right. 'Course it depends on one's definition of a shit. To think I would have run off and married him that night."

"Wouldn't you still?"

She shrugs slightly. "Depends how he explains himself."

"But if he cheats on you?"

Nodding, she scoffs, "Stupid, huh? I don't know, we'll see. Got nothing else better and he's the only one I've known, or at least loved. Do you know how lucky you are to live here?" she asks me.

We stand on the landing at the top of the stairs overlooking the beach. The air is moist, and still, gulls drift lazily above, their cackles echoing sharply.

"How many people get to spend their summers on a cliff above a lake with their own beach?"

I haven't given it a lot of thought, but I'd never thought about a lot of things before Mom's stroke.

"Back home we take trips to the ocean, but you always fight the crowds." She peers at the horizon and inhales the fresh air. "It's so peaceful." Then she suddenly cries, "Beat you to the water!" as she races down the stairs.

By the time I hit the hot sand, she is ripping her shirt off in mid-stride. Coming to a stuttered stop at the water, she bounces and hops out of her shorts, diving in naked. Upon surfacing, floating on her back, breasts exposed above the surface, she smiles. Her hair is slicked back off her face. "Drop trow and jump in!"

Morning sunlight streams through her windows, bleaching the bed. I try to recall each moment of the previous day and night, attempting to etch it into my long-term memory. I remain motionless for fear of disturbing her, afraid of her mood, afraid to threaten the balance we've achieved. Never having experienced the constancy, the physicality, I am not convinced it is important, that it means as much as I hope for. I know it can't last but can't help praying it will.

She is wrapped tightly in a sheet and facing away from me as I travel the outline of her body from her feet, up over the raised hips to her back, and end at her wild mess of blonde hair. Mom is out of my thoughts and has been since I dove into the lake yesterday.

"Never in my life … Think we should send it to the *Guinness Book of World Records*?" She flips over and faces me without taking her head off the pillow. Eye makeup is smudged, darkening her eyes with raccoon-like circles. She lifts an eyebrow.

Smiling slightly, I ask, "How about the two-day record?"

She pulls the sheet over her head and lets out a mock scream. "A machine!"

Later, emerging from the shower stall, dripping in the hallway, gazing out onto the front yard, she suggests, "Another fantasy of mine."

I take her shoulders, holding her at arm's length and scoff playfully, "What now?"

"The day, and I mean the whole day, no clothes."

I step back and gaze at her long, athletic legs, the wet, tangled hair splayed over her swollen red labia, then at her muscular stomach and pause at her firm breasts, nipples erect in the chill of the morning. "You're on."

With a giggle, she shakes her tangle of curls at me like a wet dog and races toward the living room. With me on her tail, she shoots out the porch door and descends the stairs to the beach where we sprint across the sand and dive into the cool lake without hesitation.

Upon surfacing, she cries, "Race you to the second sandbar," and churning in a frantic freestyle, I pass the first sandbar, not looking over until the light sand of the second appears. Rolling over onto my back I look back for her, but she isn't there, and worried, I quickly stand up, water reaching my chest, afraid she's drowned in the eight-foot water between the bars.

"Who you looking for?" she taunts from behind me. "I didn't think you'd ever get here."

"Holy shit! Where'd you learn to swim so fast?"

"School team. Actually, I'm not very good which proves how slow you are."

"Why aren't you any good?"

"Hell, I spent most of my time flirting with the football players in the weight room."

"I thought you were swimming."

"They have a window that looks into the pool, and we always swam by, flashing them and stuff. It's great fun."

There is a pang of tightness in my stomach, thinking of her teasing the players. I think of Dwayne for the first time and almost say something, but hold back.

After breakfast, I say, "I know a place with swinging vines."

She smirks doubtfully. "You mean like Tarzan and Jane?"

"Exactly."

She follows me into the dampness of the woods, padding across a moss-covered path that winds through tall oaks into a clearing. She pinches me on the ass as she gallops by and begins scaling the tree skillfully.

"A bit of chimpanzee in you!"

"Call me Cheetah," she laughs while inching out onto a branch.

"I think I'll stick with Jane. I think there are laws against that chimpanzee thing."

She lifts herself up lithely with the help of a branch above and grabs a vine that is looped around it. Breathless, huffing, she stands to clutch it.

"Be careful."

"Oh, didn't I tell you? I'm on the vine swinging team at school too. How far do you think I can fly?" she asks surveying the clearing. "Give me a target."

I survey the clearing, squinting into the bright sunrays cascading through intermittent openings in the forest ceiling. "See the last circle of light?"

"Not a problem, Tarzan." She bends her knees and sways back and forth to gain momentum, tugging on the vine to test its strength. A worried look flashes across her face. "What if it breaks?"

"It won't, Jane."

"Well, if Tarzan says so," she screams as she sways back one more time and then leaps. Hair flowing, taut legs wrapped around the vine, she glides serenely through the funnels of sunlight and lets go a few feet above the target, tumbling softly into the grass. Rolling onto her back, she kicked her legs into the air and screams, "That is about the best ride I've ever taken!"

"I resent that," I laugh and join her in the grass.

The first phone call at dusk is Dad. "Danny …" His voice is rough, and the immense fatigue is evident.

I brace myself and say nothing, a bit irritated that reality has smashed into my dream world.

"Are you still there?"

"Uh huh."

"It's not looking good." His words sprint out before choking on tears, followed by the anguished moan of a wounded animal—unexpected and haunting.

"But she's alive?"

His sigh is drawn out. "They don't like the turn she's taken."

"She'll pull through, Dad. She's strong."

"I thought so too. She doesn't look well. Her breathing is so shallow."

My throat closes and tears blind me.

"I can't leave her, buddy."

"You're right. You stay. I'll be fine."

"You sure?"

"I'm sure. Hug her. Tell her I love her."

His sobs rush over the phone like frantic barks.

The idea of never seeing her again makes me nauseous.

The phone is dead, and I'm gazing into the woods. The best day of my life has just ended. The crackle of the breeze in the branches is the only sound.

"Your mom?"

I turn and stare blankly at her.

"Did she?" She reaches out to me.

"Not yet." The final sentence echoes off the walls. The prior week I'd been anxiously waiting summer. Now I stand naked, staring at a woman I'd made love to for the better part of two days, and am facing the rest of my life without Mom, my best friend.

She pulls me to her chest, and we rock back and forth.

I want desperately to cry, release the pain, but something tells me that doing so, in effect, is a pronouncement of death. She doesn't want me to give up on her so easily.

I squeeze Karen and bite my quivering lip. I am Mom's link to immortality, she's told me many times, but standing in the waning light, I'm not sure I'm up to the task.

The boisterous ring of the phone startles us.

"Do you want me to get it?"

Chest tight with anticipation, I walk to it without a word. I need to do it, face whatever is to happen. If Karen answers it, I might not be able to take it from her. I pick it up on the third ring.

"Is Karen there?" The voice is deep and gruff.

With a slack frown, I slowly turn and hold it out to her.

I stop at each stair on my way to the beach, fighting to come to terms with the events. The moon peeks down from above the forest behind me and sheds a silver glow on the sand. The dark blanket of the lake is motionless and eerily silent as

I approach it. A bright display of stars twinkles over the horizon, and I watch, waiting for one to fall. Mom always tells me a shooting star signifies someone dying and I plop down in the lapping water and await the sign. She doesn't want to be a vegetable. If alive, she needs swimming, playing tennis, participating in our lives.

"Dan?"

"Mom?" But it's Karen.

"You've been down here for over an hour."

I snort. She wears the same outfit she wore when she arrived. I'm still naked.

"Dan. I'm leaving ..."

I knew as soon as I heard Dwayne's voice on the phone. After all, this has all just been a momentary event, a wonderful fantasy I'll never forget. In the moonlight, her tanned face contrasts sharply with her light curls. "How are you going?"

She hesitates, shuffling her weight back and forth nervously and avoiding my inquisitive stare. "Dwayne's up at the house."

"He came after all."

Sniffling, she nods. Are the tears sadness or happiness? "Have you ever seen a shooting star?" she asks, gazing up at the harvest of stars glittering like diamonds in the black sky, wiping a tear with the back of her hand.

"Sure."

"They're good luck, you know."

She wraps her arms around her chest, glancing up and down the shore at all the flickering lights in homes where normal everyday conversations are taking place, where children are laughing with their parents. "He wants me to marry him tonight."

"Isn't that what you want?"

"Wanted. It's what I wanted. After the last couple of days, I've realized I'm not ready for that." She takes a deep breath. "But I know I can't stay here."

As much as I want her to stay, I can't argue. Taking her in my arms, hugging her tightly, a desperate squeeze, I kiss her one last time. My arms are limp at my sides as she disappears into the dark shadows at the foot of the cliff, and I wait for a number of minutes before scaling the stairs myself.

The massive house is bathed in moonlight, many windows blankly gazing out to sea as I plod slowly across the dew-drenched front lawn. Upon entering the foyer, there is the yellow glow of one lone lamp in the living room, and I want so desperately to feel the feelings I had just weeks before, but know I've lost them forever.

I crawl into Karen's unmade bed, tossing myself into a fitful sleep immersed in her pungent, flowery scent, restlessly dreaming throughout the night about the women in my life.

Unbound

Slaidey Valheim

Beth sips her coffee, stalling for time. She mulls over her answer to the inescapable question, "So how are you and Daniel doing?" That's the go-to topic for every social occasion. Beth normally would have formulated some appropriate response hours before meeting Jules, but what she wants to say is exceptionally personal. 'Intimacy advice' falls under the taboo heading of Beth's 'acceptable conversations' topics list.

"We're okay," Beth studies her cup's lid. Some creamer is stuck in the lip.

"Beth, come on. I just regaled you with all the bullshit I've gone through dealing with my work's new, young, and completely incompetent manager. You've got to have something you want to talk about," Jules insists.

"Are you and Roy happy?" Beth attempts a transition to the topic scratching at the back of her mind.

"I'd say so … Are you and Daniel having problems?" Jules raises a little from her seat in alarm.

"No, no. Well, no. Not in the drastic sense," Beth tries to wave away her friend's concern. "It's just, your relationship with Roy is so new compared to mine and Daniel's. We were thinking of spicing it up a bit …" Beth would prefer not to get specific. She trails off and takes another sip of her drink.

"Oh, you're going to become swingers! That's fun!"

Beth chokes on her liquid caffeine. "God Jules, no!" Beth takes a quick look around the room to see if anyone noticed their outburst. No fellow customers are looking in their direction. "Could you be a bit more discrete?"

"Ha, ha, ha. Oh, it's 2017 Beth. Nobody cares. I'm just kidding!" Jules leans back in her chair; relieved Beth wasn't about to drop news of a late age pregnancy or impending divorce.

"Obviously I want things to remain," Beth twirls her hand in the air looking for the word, "secluded. Things have just gotten … I don't want to say boring," Beth frowns.

"Like you're jerking yourself off on your partner's body?" Jules offers.

"Ya." The corner of Beth's lips curl down, worried that admittance might have been insulting to Daniel. "To put it so beautifully blunt. I mean, it's fine. We've always been vanilla. I'm traditional and Daniel isn't spontaneous. But the thing is, we don't have anything else big going on in our lives. We've got a lot of extra time on our hands. Going out gets tedious … we'd rather stay inside."

"Oh Beth, my sweet Beth. I know exactly what you mean. Ed and I got like that." Beth's eyes widen. Jules never willingly talks about Ed.

"Before you ask, our sex life had nothing to do with why we divorced," Jules continues. "Actually, once we hit the point of 'fuck everything, I hate you and you hate me,' the sex got a hell of a lot better. It was liberating not to care. We tried a lot of things, and if I'm entirely honest, that kept us together a few months longer than we should have been."

"Oh, wow." Beth tries to process this new information. Beth never knew Ed personally, she'd only been told that he was some asshole Jules married too young.

"But Beth, we've watched enough rom-coms together to know what the easy next step is … *Toys*," Jules says matter-of-factly.

Beth finishes her coffee, taking one large last gulp. "I can't see Daniel wielding a toy of any sort."

"You can't go into it with that attitude! Daniel's a great guy who loves to please, so don't be hesitant. Maybe he'll step up to the plate?" Jules throws encouragement at Beth, knowing full well that Beth rarely adventures but definitely deserves to. "And don't knock it 'til you try it! I loved me a good spank on the—" Jules smacks the side of the table.

The sugar jar jiggles, and Beth's empty cup falls over.

"Jules!" This time the barista gives them a disapproving glare. Jules laughs, and Beth nearly turns to stone.

"Okay, good luck," Jules bids her friend, giving Beth's shoulder a quick fleeting squeeze before walking away.

A few moments later, Beth is left standing at the entrance of their small town's lingerie store. Beth crosses the threshold. *This isn't so bad*, Beth thinks as she examines everything nearby. The walls are lined with bras and panties she can only imagine teenagers wearing. There are push-up bras with matching thongs colored in neon stripes. *Gaudy.*

Beth pushes on. There's a young woman behind the checkout counter. "Hello," she nods toward Beth.

"Hello," Beth replies, though immediately dismissing the cashier by turning her head in the other direction. *I'd like to just explore for a bit.* Everything around the center of the store shifts to a more mature theme. There's predominantly displayed plain silk nightgowns with small see-through lace patches down the front or back, and packs upon packs of beige nylons. *I already own these.* Beth presses on. The walls of skin colored pantyhose turn into fishnet stockings, petticoats and billowy slips, into laced corsets.

Beth stops in front of a mannequin posed with hands on its hip like it disapproves of what it sees—that being if it had a head. It wears a deep violet girdle with black puffy silk material around the breasts, and slacken around the shoulders like a bar wench's top. A short expanse of stomach shows. Low rise, shiny black underwear attach with panty hooks to thigh-high lace stockings. Placed between the mannequin's hand and hip hangs an intriguing shiny toy. Something stirs inside Beth. *Oh,* Beth can't help but grin.

"Can I help you with anything ma'am?" The young teller approaches. "As you can see, we try to organize the store based on the depth of taste." She looks over Beth's shoulder to see what's captivated the woman nearly twenty years her senior.

"Do you carry a variety of sizes here, or is it slim pickings?" Beth asks absentmindedly.

"We carry more of a variety in the clothing advertised at the front of the store. There's less stock of what's kept at the back. We don't get shipments for these products as often." Beth stands there silent, eyeing the ensemble. *She doesn't think I should be back here,* Beth muses. *I don't know if I should be back here either ...*

The attendant switches her weight from one foot to another. "We have sales on the newly imported Egyptian silk nightgowns in everything from baby blue to dusted rose," the girl adds nervously. *That's the sort of thing someone my age should wear.*

"Seeing as there isn't much selection, I'd like to buy what's on this mannequin. The entire set, including that," Beth motions to the doll's wrist. "It should fit me just fine." Beth looks back at the worker hovering behind her. The young woman tries to hide her underlying shock.

"As you wish, Ma'am." Beth can't tell if her choice came from a whim, defiance at the young woman suggesting she buy otherwise, or simply madness.

"Beth?" Daniel calls as he enters the apartment. He kicks off his shoes and drops his keys in the main entrance bowl. They clang against hers. Beth's anticipation rises, she gets tingles in her chest and clutches tighter at what's in her hands.

"I'm in here!" She replies, hoping she doesn't sound anxious. *Maybe it was a mistake to try this as soon as he got home. He could be tired.*

Beth hears Daniel's socks brush against the floor. Their bedroom door is a foyer type installation, and Daniel hesitates on the other side before sliding open the panels. "You've got a surprise for me?"

Daniel enters the room with his eyes squinted and a huge smile across his face. He's always ready to laugh, it's his default response to uncomfortable situations. He isn't aiming to dismiss Beth's efforts, only to make light of the situation and ease his vulnerability to the unexpected. But not a chuckle has a chance to escape his throat before he is captivated by the sight before him. Daniel's eyebrows rise, and his jaw loosens.

Beth sits on the end of their bed. The tones of the room are pale and subdued. Daniel had it this way long before Beth moved in. He enjoys the calming aura of light bamboo hardwood and textured wallpaper of blue-gray quartz. The setting throws a hard contrast to Beth's presence.

Beth sits neatly with her hands behind her back. Her knees are together but not tightly, raised above the bed level, heightened by the two-inch heels. Straight brown hair cascades over her shoulders and frames her bosom. Her breasts are pushed up, neatly rounded and peeking out from her corset-styled top. She kept her makeup simple, however, a little mascara with pale translucent lip gloss. A woman that appears to belong in this room and an outfit that doesn't.

Her shoulders are lax and display no tension. Once Daniel entered the room, all her apprehensions seemed silly. *Why should I be nervous? It's Daniel.* He loves Beth to the moon and back. He'd do anything for her. Beth surely has nothing to worry about. Daniel, on the other hand, might.

Daniel blinks, not knowing what to say. Beth counts the passing seconds. *I'll start things off.*

There's a clinking noise behind her. "I bought something for you." She can't bring herself to say 'us.' She presents the handcuffs in front of her. Two cufflinks in her palms, fanned by neatly manicured fingernails.

It would normally be said, 'Daniel's face faltered, and a mischievous grin spread across his face,' but this is not the case. Daniel merely blinks.

He looks at the handcuffs.

He looks at his wife.

He gingerly raises his hands to receive the metallic gift. He shakes his head to clear his faltering brain and focus on what he's expected to do. "Okay," is all he can muster.

Taking the queue, Beth scoots back on the bed and lays down. She raises her hands above her head and rests them on the pillows, wrist to wrist. Beth tilts her head to the side, trying to invite him to join her. "Coming?" she prompts.

"Ya," Daniel sputters. He approaches the end of the bed and crawls toward her. Beth opens her legs so he might have an easier time getting close to her. Her suggestive pose makes Daniel pause for a millisecond before continuing to progress on his daunting mission.

Daniel inches his way over her. Left hand, right hand, on either side of her torso, until they're face to face. He can't reach her hands though, not while supporting himself with his own. "Uh," he lifts his knees over her thighs and continues to shimmy up.

Beth stares at Daniel's bellybutton as he tries to use the handcuffs. His shirt droops onto her forehead. *Why didn't he undress?* Daniel closes the cuffs around her wrists so lightly that she could squeeze her hands out if she tried.

Without repositioning his legs, Daniel lowers his face back to Beth's. He smiles awkwardly. His body seems so small curled around her torso like this. She can't feel any part of him. He's being exceptionally careful not to make contact.

Daniel goes in for a kiss then withdraws. "Heh," he chuckles. Beth's eyebrows knit together. Daniel lowers his lips. He pecks her over and over. He's not closing his eyes and now neither is she. A few times he puts great pressure on her mouth and yet, does not move his own.

Beth tries to part her lips, take the reins, but it feels wrong. *That's not my role right now,* she tries to convince herself. *I got HIM the cuffs.*

After a few minutes, Daniel lifts himself away from Beth. His face is sympathetic. "Sorry Beth, it's just … I've had a long day of work." A part of her wants to believe him, but it's such an obvious lie.

"S-stupid," escapes Beth's lips.

"Excuse me?" Daniel asks, hurt.

Beth's face contorts. *That wasn't supposed to be out loud. I don't even know which of us I think is stupider.* "I just meant, it was stupid of me to do this. I should have known you'd be exhausted," she lies too.

"Oh." Daniel looks away, brewing with insecurity.

"The handcuff keys are on the desk," Beth tries to add lightly.

"What?" Daniel seems lost in a haze.

"The keys are on the desk," Beth repeats sternly.

"Right! Sorry." Daniel scrambles off the bed and snatches the keys. Beth sits up and swings her legs over the bed toward him. She presents her wrists before her. Daniel gives her a wane smile as he fumbles with the locks. Beth catches the undone handcuffs, feeling Daniel's unwillingness to take them into his possession.

"I'll just go have a shower?" Daniel says, posing it as a question.

"Of course, honey." Beth gives him a nod and one last smile before he leaves the room, trying to reassure Daniel there are no hard feelings.

Once she hears the water running in the bathroom, she flops on the bed, discontented. *I guess I have to change out of this,* she accepts reluctantly.

Beth sits in the dark at the desk in their bedroom. She crawled out of the sheets at two a.m., unable to sleep. She considers last night a disaster. *He didn't like it. I need to do my homework. The outfit wasn't the problem, it couldn't have been. I looked sexier than I have in years.* Beth doesn't even humor the possibility of the thought. She likes her new outfit far too much.

Beth fires up their shared desktop computer. Daniel supposedly only uses it for work, but Beth suspects otherwise. Beth is not naive—as Julia pointed out—but she needs to be willing to cross her self-imposed line of acceptability. She knows some things, but she hasn't explored. Beth types "P" into the search browser, and it reveals Daniel's porn sites.

Typing out the rest of the basic URL so what shows up in the suggested search bar are previously visited pathways. *This is the most recent, or most watched, I suppose.* Beth adjusts her earbuds and clicks the top result.

Hastily tapping the play button to pause, it buffers. She takes time to process the title, "Dominatrix Teacher Knows You've Been a Bad Boy."

Beth hasn't seen much porn and doesn't indulge in it herself. Sunday school sermons about the sinful nature of masturbation stuck with her long after she lost her religion, among other things.

Beth scrolls down the comments. She's not logged into a profile, so she has no way of knowing whether any of them belong to Daniel. Aside from the usual, 'This is so hot' comments, there is a sprinkle of niche specific ones. "I've been so bad!", "Punish me!", "I submit!", *Oh, my.*

Beth goes back to the video and hits play. For twenty minutes a woman in tight spandex berates and hits around the camera with a ruler. Beth recoils from the perspective the video presents. *People like this? I'll try another, maybe it just isn't the right one for me.* Scrolling the sidebar, Beth finds one of a couple role-playing. *This seems better.* Then she finds a POV from the dominatrix. *Alright,* Beth lets out a sigh of relief. *I can do that.*

Beth sits in her chair and thinks. She feels a bit otherworldly like she sees herself outside of her body. It's almost time for Daniel to wake up. *What should I do next? I want—* Beth stops her train of thought and detours. Her upbringing reins her desires back into the line of respectability. *I can be like those women,* Beth decides. *For my husband,* she adds.

She types, "Dominatrix" into the search engine, but that's not going to be enough. Typing one word will elicit the same sort of videos she just watched for hours on end. *Classes? Classes.* "Dominatrix Classes," Beth enters.

There are a lot of results, some of the porn sites were weeded out, and yet many still appear under the tags. Beth opens one that looks like an introductory video attached to a local Craigslist ad. "Greetings ladies. So, you want to learn to be Dominatrix?" Pause. Beth looks at the digital clock. *I don't have time for this.* Beth looks back at Daniel, snoring quietly. *I'll favorite it, wait, no. Shit.* If she favorites it, then Daniel will see. *UGH.* Annoyed, Beth ignores the video, copies the contact info and opens her email.

What do I say? It's six am. "Hi, I want to—" Beth contemplates the wording. *What do I want to do? Spice up my sex life? That's cheesy.* "My name is Beth. I tried bringing handcuffs into our bedroom. My partner didn't seem to like it. I found Dominatrix themes in his porn watch history. I would like to do that for him ..."

No that's so needy. "I can be that for him with training. Please teach me."

Beth backs up one more time. *No 'please,' this is a business email.* "When is your earliest opening?" *End on a question, make them respond.* Beth has been in marketing long enough to know some key communication tricks.

She sends the email. *AH!* A ping hits her. Beth has earbuds in, and she startles. She darts her head back to Daniel to make sure she didn't wake him. He's okay. She opens the message.

"You realize I only book one session per week? It will cost cash up front. I don't like to have my time wasted."

No, Beth hadn't known that. She didn't check any of the additional information or watch the informational video. Daniel rolls over in his sleep and mumbles. Beth fervently clacks her fingers across the keyboard. "I'll bring the money. When?" Beth doesn't have time to be anything but blunt.

"Today at one p.m. I will teach you to be a Dominatrix. You will come, and you will learn." Attached is an address.

"I'll be there." Beth means for her reply to be courteous, though terribly short. It'd be awful to expect someone and have them never show up.

"I know you will. One p.m. sharp. I will not open my door after. Wear something appealing. If you reply to this email, I will not teach you. This is the end of our conversation." *A bit rude. I wasn't just trying to get the last word in … She seems like she's the kind of person who needs to,* Beth decides.

Beth looks at the screen, not quite sure what to do. She's been conditioned to act grateful, at least to say thank you, but her efforts are condemned. *Would she really do that? Leave me standing at the door?* Beth sits and ponders. Their exchange had been short and to the point. Beth hadn't been friendly herself, but she also didn't appreciate the Dom's tone.

Beth deletes the email chain and shuts off the computer. She crawls into bed with Daniel and tries to imagine what this afternoon will entail. Beth's always been a planner, she takes comfort in the sense of control. This sudden adventurous spurt has her a bit off kilter, but excited.

Beth looks at her watch and notes it's 12:55 p.m. She took the message in the email to heart. To not be punctual is intolerable by her standards anyway.

She stares at her watch. It's getting so close. The second-hand ticks.

Seven.

Six.

Five.

Four.

Three.

Two.

One.

The door opens. On the dot. A sense of slight intimidation washes over her.

"Come in," a voice beckons. Beth steps into her trainer's apartment. Her host shuts the door behind her and leads Beth to the living room furniture. A love seat sits across from an ornate armchair, the two separated by a storage-type wooden coffee table. The woman is beautiful in a natural way, yet her makeup further accentuates her eyes and lips. She has dark skin and hair that's braided down her back. She wears a simple black cocktail dress and strapped heels. "Tell me your name."

"My name is Beth." *Although, I already said that in the email.*

"That's an old name," the Dominatrix says with a hint of boredom.

"My parents were Christian," Beth offers, immediately defensive.

"My name is Miss Vixie."

"Uh, okay. Hello, Miss Vixie."

"Refrain from saying 'uh.' It's unappealing. Do you have the money?" Beth's face flushes red, and she frowns.

Rude. Let's just get on with this. Beth hands Vixie a discrete envelope. Miss Vixie tucks it in her bra. "Okay. Well, you know why I came here," Beth presses, hoping to get things started and not waste her own precious time.

"Tell me why you came here."

"What?" Beth repeatedly blinks, rather confused. *This isn't the wrong apartment …*

"Tell me why you came here," Miss Vixie repeats.

Beth stares at Vixie and creases her forehead. *You read my email less than twelve hours ago.*

"If you don't tell me, how can I help?" Vixie adds.

"I brought handcuffs into the bedroom, and it didn't work out," Beth gives a little shrug, trying to act casual.

"How so?"

"Daniel was really hesitant."

"Daniel is your lover?"

"Husband." *There, now I've repeated every-thing.*

"Hmmm." Miss Vixie makes a sound in the back of her throat. "I see." She strokes her cheek lightly in thought. "Did you wear what I instructed?"

"Yes."

"Take the coat off then." Beth scans for a coat rack. "Take it off when I tell you to," Vixie insists.

Beth unbuttons her knee-length jacket and lets it fall onto the armchair behind her. Beth wore the top and her panties but this time with regular nylons, ones she wears every day with her button-up floral sundresses, as well as her usual penny loafers. "That outfit will do," Vixie sighs. Beth's lips tighten. "Do you have equipment with you?"

"Equipment?"

"Whatever you tried with your partner who didn't like it?" Vixie states in a condescending tone.

"Handcuffs," Beth reiterates, getting agitated. *In less than a minute you've forgotten that I specifically said handcuffs, and you don't remember Daniel's name or that he's my husband?*

"So, you didn't bring them?" Vixie asks for confirmation.

"Well, no," Beth admits.

"Disappointing. In a drawer under the coffee table, there's an instrument. Retrieve it."

Beth sits down and tentatively pulls the handle under the wooden table between them. There's something in the space, a thin rod attached to many long tassel-like leather strips.

Beth pulls it out of the drawer. "Hold the grip in your dominant hand." Beth grasps the end and slips the strap over her slender wrist. She looks back at her instructor. Vixie shows no emotion. She's not even looking at Beth. Sitting across from one another, Beth carefully sets the flog over her knee.

Vixie's eyes slowly wander back to appraise Beth. "Your outfit looks abhorrent compared to your face."

Beth nearly chokes in surprise. "Excuse me?"

"Stand up." Beth frowns and retains eye contact, defiant and unwilling to move. Her mentor gets to her feet. "I said stand up." Beth puts her hands on her legs and pushes herself to stand across from Miss Vixie. "That wasn't so hard, now was it? Do you have shoes to go with that outfit?"

"Yes."

"Why didn't you wear them?"

"It wasn't practical." *What's with the stupid questions? How was I supposed to wear or bring these things with me? I ran errands before I came here. I had a chat with the mailman dressed like this underneath, and that wasn't bad enough? This woman has no common sense.*

"When are heels ever practical," Miss Vixie muses before her face changes and her tone becomes serious. "We wear them because it makes us attractive. You need to know what can make you seem more attractive. Tall, slender figures. Straight backs. Big tits. Voluptuous butts. Thick thighs. A pretty face. Play on your assets. You could add height with heels. If you don't, you're at a dis-advantage."

"At a disadvantage, to whom?" *The mailman? Only Daniel will ever see me dressed like this.*

Miss Vixie scoffs. "I suppose you don't want a vague answer. It puts you at a disadvantage to every single person who could be looking up to you. Show me your accessory."

It takes Beth a moment to realize 'accessory' referred to the limp noodles hanging from the rod in her hand. She raises it between them. "Consider this another accessory. The clothes and toys you buy and wear are accessories to enhance your body—your weapon. However, I am not like you; naive. I am Miss Vixie. I'm experienced and uninhibited. I don't need such juvenile props anymore, and I do not care for stuttering imbeciles who don't know what they want."

"Do you mean me?" Beth asks, shocked. Vixie raises her eyebrow in acknowledgment. "I know what I want. I came here to learn to please my husband."

"And you expect to do it dressed like that?" Vixie provokes.

Beth looks down at herself. *Does it all seem ridiculous now? Should it?*

"Your muffin top is showing. It's the least attractive quality in a woman, and you're accentuating it. But that's not the problem. You look very good for your age, but nothing matches. Your face and your legs belong to a different person than your torso. You look abominable."

"I don't," Beth breathes. "And this lingerie was a top-selling item at—"

"Justifying yourself based on others? Your outfit makes you look like a confused child."

They're standing face to face across from each other. "I am not a child."

"Aren't you though?" Miss Vixie looks ready to laugh.

"No." *I'm at least a decade older than you!*

"Do you really believe that?"

"I look damn good for a forty-year-old!" Beth spurts.

"I don't understand why you haven't done anything with your face or hair. The outfit, fine, but your face is your identifier. It's what people look at. There's nothing. You're naked."

Beth is shaking. "I had to walk all the way here. I wasn't going to dress to the hilt. That wouldn't be … humble."

"I don't see your point. You didn't want people to look at you with any semblance of desire or respect? Is that what you're telling me?" Beth doesn't quite know what to say. "We're done here. I can't teach someone like you." Vixie turns and walks to the other side of the room to get a drink from her liquor cabinet.

"Wait," Beth squeaks, trying to find her voice.

"I don't speak mouse," Vixie's words are like knives.

Beth clears her throat. "You can't be like that."

"Oh, I can't?"

"I paid good money for this," Beth explains.

"Good money? Are you in such financial trouble you consider that small sum good money?" Vixie talks over her shoulder as she pours a drink.

"No. That's not the point! Give me my money back." All the muscles in Beth's body tense and before she knows what she's doing, she smacks the coffee table with the flog.

"No," Vixie responds casually, entirely unperturbed.

"You have to," Beth states.

"What are you going to do about it? It's my word over yours. There's no way to prove services weren't rendered. Do you really want to get the police involved, advertising that you got scammed on a Dominatrix class? Someone who won't even wear heels or makeup in public?" Vixie sips her drink.

Beth smacks the coffee table with her accessory harder. "You will give me my money back!"

"Oh, will I?"

"Yes."

"Why?"

"Because I came here to learn," Beth yells. "And look at me when I'm talking to you!"

"Learn what exactly?" Vixie puts down her glass and turns back around to look at Beth's unraveling. Her face is stern, flog in hand, legs stiff.

"I already told you! What is wrong with you? You just keep running the conversation in circles, asking stupid questions! Come back over here!" The leather tassels whip against the wooden centerpiece. Miss Vixie walks over slowly, looking amused, and resumes her spot sitting across from Beth.

"My strategy as a Dominatrix is to ignore my clients and insult them. I make them repeat themselves, so they know what they have to say is so unimportant, I can't be bothered to remember a word of it. I use this persona when I teach classes to women seeking to be a Dominatrix to weed out those unfit for the job. Your emails were commanding, but after observing who I assumed to be you through your profiles, I had my doubts. Did you have fire or were you just in a hurry? I wanted to see if you'd buckle; submit to my harassment or stand up for yourself? It's always interesting to see whether people are susceptible to both sides of the situation too. I like both, so I can either show people what to do or let them experiment their own strategies on me. You aren't the same. Being treated like a sub makes you very displeased."

Beth's muscles loosen. *Wait, she's not a bitch with a hole in her head?*

"Which is an odd hypocrisy because you present yourself in that category. Although, I see that only you are allowed to inconvenience or squander your own potential." Vixie bites her lip, thinking over her next monologue.

"If you want this session to go well, then I need you to stop lying to me, Beth."

Beth looks back at her, puzzled. Not only did Vixie's entire demeanor swing from obnoxious to patient, but Beth didn't know what she's talking about.

"You didn't come here to 'please your husband.' You could do that easily with a surprise morning blowjob. You came here to please yourself. You chose this means of execution. Someone not inclined to roleplay never makes it this far. They don't put in the effort to make an appointment let alone yell commands at me, or scuff up my furniture."

Beth's eyes widen as she's hit with a pang of guilt.

Miss Vixie lets out a small laugh and waves her hand, "It's fine. But I need you to look at yourself, Beth. Look at what you're wearing. Hear the things you've said to me. You don't need to make excuses for wanting to feel sexy or powerful. If that's who you are, you don't need to hide it behind acceptable looking clothes in fear of what other's might think. Sure, you might only want to use your full Dominatrix persona in the bedroom with your husband, but that doesn't mean you can't let that confidence seep into other aspects of your life.

"This lifestyle is all or nothing. You liberate yourself, or you don't. Look at me. I do whichever my clients need because I like it. I can be respectable and naughty. They aren't mutually exclusive. Wear what you want. Be true to yourself. It's about empowerment, and to me, you look extremely repressed." Miss Vixie refers to Beth's mismatched clothes and mortification toward displaying any of her own assets. Vixie is finished with her speech.

Beth sinks to the couch behind her and lets the words wash over her. They sit in silence for some time. The teachings of Beth's parents echo in the back of her head. Indecency and respectability always had an opposing existence; finding joy in sexuality was shameful. *Then why do I enjoy it? I never gave it a thought before, but I am drawn to it. Now … Of course, look where I'm sitting! I came all this way! I want to be here. I must want to express myself in this way.*

Vixie tilts her head and continues in a soft voice. "Even under pressure and anger you remained fairly composed, which is the mark of a good Dominatrix. I'd like you to show me your fire, in a calculated way."

For some reason, Beth is panting. Everything laid on the table, she feels exhilarated at having passed the test.

"Now what are you going to do if I don't refund your money? Will you spank me, Beth?"

Beth grips the flog tightly in her hand. "Yes."

"Well, I'm not giving your money back," Miss Vixie confirms.

"Then bend over the couch," Beth's eyes glow, and she stands with a spurt of confidence.

"Yes, ma'am," Vixie replies with a grin. "My safe word is 'unbound.'"

Later when Daniel gets home from work, he hears, "Come in here."

Daniel pauses even longer on the other side of the bedroom door than before. He's thinking about their last attempt, afraid to under-preform or let Beth down. He wishes they could wait a few more days before trying again, but Beth is calling the shots now.

"Don't keep me waiting."

Daniel enters the bedroom. Beth is on the edge of the bed, but this time is different; this time she straddles it, legs parted, hands in front of her holding the handcuffs dangling by their chain. Her hair is pulled into a tight, high ponytail. She bats long lashes surrounded by smoky eyeshadow. Her lips are glistening, black and plump. Deep purple fingernails tap on metal.

"Beth?"

"Call me Lady Bethany," she instructs. Beth stands and takes purposeful strides from the end of the bed to the side, never breaking eye contact. Her heels clack against the hardwood floors. "Undress and get on the bed," she commands. She jingles the handcuffs and pulls them taut; loops around her thumbs as she watches Daniel comply.

Beth wanders into the bedroom after a relaxing shower. She's in a fuzzy robe, teasing her hair with a towel. Although Daniel has since put on his boxers, he's still lying sprawled on the bed.

"Are you okay, honey?"

"Ya," Daniel exhales. "I'm great," he admits, sounding dazed.

"I'm glad you enjoyed yourself," she takes a seat beside him. "After yesterday, I was concerned you really didn't like the handcuffs."

"I didn't like them?"

"Well, ya. It looked like you weren't into the whole thing," Beth shrugs.

"Oh." Daniel murmured, his mouth twisting in thought. "I was having a hard time because you looked so unhappy."

Beth makes a noise in her throat to encourage an explanation.

"Getting tied down didn't look like your idea of fun. I don't know. I didn't think I was doing anything right, too. I just wanted to please you. You seemed uncomfortable, unlike today." He grins. "I can't say I mind getting restrained."

"I was into it, I was just playing the wrong part." Beth laid her head down beside him and reviewed her last few days. *Miss Vixie was right. Did the saleswoman push me to buy the outfit in defiance or had I already decided? Am I drawn to cuffs, with absolutely no intention of being subject to them? Did I watch all those Dominatrix videos in unwilling admiration?* Her mind might overthink, but her body knew exactly what it needed.

Lady Bethany now makes no excuses for what she wants.

Contributors

C. W. Bigelow

After receiving his B.A. in English from Colorado State University, C.W. Bigelow lived in nine northern states, both east and west, before moving south to the Charlotte, NC area.

His short stories and poems have most recently appeared in Foliate Oak Literary Magazine, Potluck, Dirty Chai, The Flexible Persona, Literally Stories and Compass Magazine, FishFood Magazine, Poydras Review, Five2One, Yellow Chair Review, Shoe Music Press, Crack the Spine, Sick Lit Magazine, Brief Wilderness with a story forthcoming in Poydras Review.

JL Higgs

J L Higgs' short stories typically focus on life from the perspective of a black American. The primary goal of his writings is to create a greater understanding between racial, ethnic, and religious groups in America.

He has been published in various magazines such as Indiana Voice Journal, Black Elephant, The Writing Disorder, Literally Stories, Contrary Magazine, and The Remembered Arts Journal. He's been nominated for a Pushcart Prize.

He and his wife currently reside outside of Boston as do their son and daughter.

You can follow him on Facebook: https://www.facebook.com/JL-Higgs-ArtistWriter-1433711619998262

Dallas Hunter

Dallas received her Bachelor's Degree in English. She has been writing since the 5th grade when she wrote her first novel for NaNoWriMo.

Living in Albuquerque, New Mexico with her husband and dog, Dallas primarily writes what she likes to read, but also likes experimental forms of literature.

Arielle Jones

Arielle Jones has earned a Bachelor's Degree in Creative Writing from San Francisco State University. She is currently an MFA candidate at Fresno State University.

She has been a fiction reader for The Normal School as well as a reader for the Levine Prize Poetry Contest.

Robert Nelis

Robert Nelis began his writing career as he commuted to and from his job as a municipal official in Chicago suburbs, creating characters and laying out plots as he drove and sketching them out later. Now retired, he enjoys having time to write the stories he planned over his twenty-seven years of commuting.

Rob received a Master's Degree in Urban Planning and Policy from the University of Illinois where he also served as adjunct faculty. He lives in Chicago with his wife of forty-two years in a 110-year-old house and enjoys his four grandchildren.

Slaidey Valheim

Slaidey contributes in her spare time to an online magazine called The Artifice.

Other Works from Temptation Press

Summer Fling: Tales of Seduction
Kiss & Tell

Coming Soon
from Temptation Press

Choices

Dreams Can Come True

A Note from the Publisher

How to Thank a Contributor

Dear Reader,

Everyone at Temptation Press would like to thank you for reading *Private Lessons*. If you would like to thank a particular contributor, the best way is to leave a review for them. You may do so by leaving one on our Goodreads page, under the title, *Private Lessons*, by using the link below:

http://www.goodreads.com/TemptationPress

and be sure to mention the contributor directly.

Why leave a review? Reviews help budding authors build their credibility in the book industry. By posting a review on Goodreads, you help other readers find new authors they may wish to follow, and you never know, your review may end up on an author's website one day.

Friend us on Goodreads:
https://www.goodreads.com/TemptationPress

Visit our website:
http://www.TemptationPress.com